A Killer fc

John Gardner

First published by Northumberland Press Limited, 1975
This edition published by Endeavour Press Ltd, 2014

For my friend Maureen Rissik

Table of Contents

The kinge then sent his jester forthe,
No matter he was wronge,
To telle the peeple he dide neede,
A killman for a songe.

The Ballad of the Kinge and the Jester, ANON, *c* 1320.

I - INTRO

Vamp 'till ready

James Gest was no Jack Jones, nor was he a Tony Bennett: and he knew it. Centred in the pool of light on the stage of the London Palladium, smooth in the midnight-blue velvet suit, he smiled acceptance of the uninspired, ragged, applause.

True, he was not unknown. There was plenty of exposure - London, Paris, New York, even Rome. Last year an offer from Vegas had fallen through at the last moment. At thirty-six, Gest knew he was never going to make the colossal international scene that always appeared to marginally elude him.

"Thank you," he murmured into the mike. "Now, it's time to say goodbye."

The MD raised his baton, bringing in the strings, shimmering low as Gest continued to speak.

"Thank you for making this a good trip for me, and tonight a special memory."

He closed his spot - the end of the first half of supporting acts for the name comedian who had been rocking them for the last three weeks - in the same way each night.

The tremolo rose, sliding into the first bars of what he had always hoped a large cognoscenti would, one day, immediately recognise as the Gest signature tune - *Whenever I leave you.*

And,
Whenever I leave you,
I will return,
And know,
That my heart will always show,
That I'll never really leave you
Again.

Five hundred dollars he had paid for the lyric and arrangement, six years ago. Christ, it was banal; the guy had conned him.

On the last word his voice dipped, then swooped up, caressing the note until it dropped into silence. Why in hell could he not have worked on his own individual style? This was pure imitation JJ. Even to the final spoken -

"Goodnight. God bless."

The orchestra switched, up-tempoing the song, a loud and romantically happy crescendo as he walked quietly from the stage. But their hearts were not in it: the volume dropped and everything petered out. James Gest breathed a sigh of relief that this was his last night in London. He felt he could do without London for a while - cold, damp, crowded, dirty London. Screw it.

The stagehands took no notice as he walked slowly in the direction of his dressing room, lighting a cigarette. Tomorrow, Paris.

His twenty-five percenter, Lou Castervermentes, who called himself manager, agent, roadie and PR man, was leaning against the wall by the dressing room, chatting up a leggy brunette from the chorus line.

Castervermentes had been with him for nine or ten years now. That, Gest thought, did not help. Castervermentes looked what he was, flashy: flashy Latin American with too many gold fillings when he smiled, and not enough charm when things did not go well. As Gest came close, Castervermentes lifted a hand to remove the cigar butt from his mouth. His fingernails were dirty.

"The man's here," he said, throwing it and turning quickly back to the girl.

"Then there'll be work, won't there?" Gest did not smile.

The manager turned and looked at him, almost with contempt.

"My kind of work?"

He did not expect an answer, turning quickly to the girl again.

Gest nodded and went into the dressing room.

Caesar Chiliman was short, fat like a slug, and gave the impression that he filled the bulk of the room - a trick of personality which, in reality, had little do with his size.

He sat on the one decent chair and Gest ignored him as he entered, walking over to the table and filling a clean glass from the gold-top bottle of milk he had bought on his way to the theatre. He drank half of the glass, topped it up, turned and leaned against the wall looking at Chiliman.

"James," Chiliman did not move a muscle, except for the smile, and he only did that with his lips, the hooded eyes hardly looking at Gest. "James, it's good to see you." His expression was at loggerheads with the words.

"What's on?"

"Work. Money. It's been a while."

"Only a few months, Caesar. Last December, or perhaps you've forgotten."

"I don't forget anything connected with our relationship, James."

"You can't afford to forget. So what is it?"

"The usual."

"Well, I didn't think you were coming on with a fat contract for me to babysit for the Osmonds. You been home lately, Caesar, or are they still looking for you?"

Chiliman's mouth twisted as though he was gathering saliva.

"I shall be able to go soon now, James. Are you 13 interested in the work or do I have to get myself some new boys?"

"If it's here, in London, there's no chance. I leave for Paris in the morning."

"For a two week spot at *Le Nostradamus*. My job is intelligence, you know."

"Yes, two lousy weeks at that over-priced fleapit and whore shop."

"You won't refuse the money." Chiliman gave an unpleasant, wheezing laugh. "Nor mine."

Gest tipped the remainder of the milk down his throat and wiped off his mouth. "So?"

"So nothing. You can still raise a team in Paris?"

"I can raise a team anywhere. No sweat."

The fat man nodded, then reached inside the breast pocket of his shapeless grey jacket, removing a neatly folded piece of paper.

"This is a list of various people who will be attending an International Security Conference in Paris over the next ten days," he passed the paper across to Gest, who took it without looking. "Names and the hotels where they will be staying. Only two need concern you. The last pair on the list."

Gest unfolded the paper and glanced down to the bottom of the closely typed page. The hotel at which they were staying was recorded as the

Baltimore, 88 bis Avenue Kleber 16e. The names were James George Mostyn and Brian Ian Oakes.

"Can do?" asked Chiliman.

"No problem. As long as the price is right, there's no problem at all."

II - REPRISE

Return to the first section of a composition

"Even my bloody face looks like yesterday," Boysie Oakes said aloud, regarding himself in the mirror, preening and turning his head to get alternate profile views. In the old days, the left - his Mona Lisa side as some woman had once put it - was always considered his best. Now, Boysie was not so sure. "Face like yesterday," he sulked. "Yesterday's bloody man."

Indeed a large number of yesterday's memories surrounded Brian Ian Oakes. True, the flat was not as large or palatial as the one he had once occupied off Chesham Place, yet it was undeniable luxury compared to the hovel in which he had been forced to live during the past two years of relative inactivity.

Boysie sloshed Aqua Manda (For Men) Pre-Electric over his jowls, regarding the fast-appearing crows' feet around his eyes with a certain sadness, clicked on the Remington cordless shaver, and began to run it over his cheeks. The left corner of his mouth twitched slightly - a sign, as he well knew, of approaching nerves.

Many familiar sensations were crowding in. Through the mirror, for instance, he could see the old and battered tan Revelation suitcase lying open where he had left it on the floor of the living room, its patina of hotel labels a constant reminder of the days when he had worked exclusively for the Department of Special Security, back in the stimulating, seductive sixties.

That was a time, Boysie reflected, when life had been brim full-overflowing with fun and death and disaster: a period when Special Security, mainly in the shape of the oily slick Colonel James George Mostyn, had employed him as an agent - a liquidating agent, designed, quite literally, to cut down security risks. They had even called him the Liquidator, though he was also known by a number of other uncomplimentary names - the chop-merchant, the waste-disposal unit, and the killer-diller: names which hardly went with Boysie's personality, for he was, in reality, the gentlest of men with a streak of anxiety which would have done credit to a highly-strung squirrel.

It was undeniable, though, that over the years Boysie had hardened. The old anxieties still occasionally unearthed themselves, but the days with Special Security had taught him much about the world and human nature; and later, when he had slithered from job to job in the cold jungle outside the government-protected department, Boysie discovered that his soft centre was getting calloused.

The odd thing, he thought, switching off the shaver and looking himself straight in the eyes - cold, ice-blue and clear as ever - was that since leaving Special Security he had never quite rid himself of his former puppet-master, Mostyn, the one man Boysie adored to loathe.

It was a long time now since he had first set eyes on the iniquitous Mostyn, during the liberation of Paris when their paths had crossed so accidentally and irrevocably.

On that particular morning Boysie had been lost - disorientated in charge of a tank. On the other hand Mostyn was fighting for his life, trapped in a cul-de-sac at the end of one of those deep-cover operations taken on by the Department in those days.

The arm of coincidence may well be out of proportion; in the case of Boysie and Mostyn it became one of life's more gruesome little jokes: Oakes advancing, looking for street names, free from his lost tank, with a Colt automatic loaded in his paw; Mostyn spotting him as the two Nazi agents moved in for the kill; Boysie jerking at the shout; the gun going off twice and the Nazis lying dead on the cobbles.

It was all a terrible accident, but the sharp little Mostyn, catching the icy look of terror in Boysie's eyes, was ready to misinterpret the signs and had his saviour marked down for a cold killer in less time than it takes to slit a chicken's gizzard.

It was years later when Mostyn, now promoted to Second-in-Command of the Department, had need of someone like the Boysie he had fashioned in his mind. When the two finally came together, Boysie, like the middle-aged man accused of rape, was too flattered to deny the deadly talents with which Mostyn now invested him.

So began an uncertain and deceitful marriage in which Mostyn, on behalf of the Department, handed out the murderous assignments to Boysie together with the commodity which Oakes needed most - pounds sterling, dollars, marks, francs, escudos, gold bricks. It did not matter how it came, but the more there was, the more Boysie needed. Money, like all habit-forming drugs, is easy when you start, but very hard to handle once you are mainlining. Boysie who had guilt problems if he stepped on an ant, soon found the going tough, and so the honeymoon with the ratty, uncompromising, omniscient Mostyn was over, and the small colonel soon became, in Boysie's mind, a two-headed monster - at one and the same time his provider and tormentor.

When the Department was reorganised, during the Madrigal fiasco, Boysie was still not able to shake himself free from Mostyn, and since then they had worked together in a private capacity, and, two years ago there was the terrifying fiasco concerning the pirate airline, when Boysie had found himself a business partner with the greasy little Mostyn. Now he was at it again. The new flat, regular salary, the perks all came from government sources and, like an old refrain, Mostyn pulled the strings.

He slapped aftershave onto his electrically-barbered cheeks, winced slightly, and began to pack his toilet gear into a long imitation calf receptacle, a one-time Christmas gift from the luscious Elizabeth, his steady bed and board partner during the halcyon days of life with the Department.

Jimmy Young prattled from the radio.

"What's the bloody recipe today, Jim?" squeaked Boysie, fighting back. "Fillet D'Oakes sans paddles? Or Stuffed Boysie à la bourgeoise?"

But it was ten in the morning and J. Young gave way for the news-disaster, crises, pollution, ecological despair, energy wind-down.

The world, thought Boysie profoundly, was gradually running out of steam: eventually its engines would flame out and it would go hurtling into space, like some huge jet with fuel starvation.

The thought made him swallow. He was flying to Paris that morning, and Boysie still could not conquer the fear of being launched into the air in a grumbling winged monster. The habit was, he considered, more dangerous now than when the idiotic Wilbur and Orville had first been foolish enough to take to wings at Kitty Hawk. Sod Wilbur and sod Orville.

The anxiety increased as he completed packing, checked the little Baby Browning-25 automatic pistol which he always carried when working, dropped it on top of his neatly folded pyjamas, and locked his case. Why was he going to Paris? The answer was inevitable: Mostyn was why he was going.

***

"Like taking iced lollies from mixed infants, old Boysie boy," Mostyn had said, Laning superciliously against the door of the bedsitter situated in tile crummier part of the Earl's Court Road.

"Why me?" Boysie heard himself say.

He could have done without the interlocutor bit really: he had heard it all before.

"Let me come in, laddie, and I'll explain."

It had been almost four years since Boysie had seen Mostyn. Not that the colonel had changed much. He was short with clean smooth upper-class features, as though he had been incubated in the hot-house of some large mansion in the shires. The tight curls were more grey, the movements more precise, the nose more sensitive.

Boysie opened the door and allowed his old superior to place his immaculately shod feet onto the worn carpet.

Mostyn looked around the room, a certain amount of pain reflecting in his eyes, and the nose wrinkled as though assailed by some obnoxious stench.

"Not very pretty, Boysie. Not very pretty at all."

"Well, things haven't been going too well."

"I do know." Mostyn gave him a look usually reserved for idiot children. "Freelance private eyes not all that much in demand, are they? And you did rather cock up that divorce thing with Mrs. Hotlips."

"Hotchkiss," corrected Boysie. "What do you know about Mrs. Hotchkiss?"

"I've got eyes, laddie. All over the scandal sheets, wasn't it? Lady employs you to watch her amorous old man and he does you as the co-respondent. Not clever, Oakesie, not clever at all."

"How was I to know he would come back? He'd been running true to form. He was always out till ten on Wednesdays."

Mostyn gave his monkey-like snigger. "Came a purler, lad. A right purler. I don't care for your wallpaper." Boysie tried to summon fragments of sarcastic wit. "Bloody beggars can't be bloody choosers, can they?"

"It's sad," Mostyn had removed a pristine handkerchief from his breast pocket and dusted off a chair before using it. "Sad that you should come to this."

"If you tell me you want to take me away from it all again, I'll thump you."

"I think not. I can take you away from it all - yet again." Mostyn's hand came up. Dangling from his fingers was a key. "Forty-six Ormsby Court, Ken High Street," he said with a leer. "All yours, son. One hundred quid a week, tax free, run of the spare grumble in the typing pool, and transport."

For a couple of seconds, Boysie stopped breathing. After what he had been through concerning vacuums in the wallet, it was a king's ransom. Common sense told him to grab. Experience warned prudence.

"Not the airline thing again?" He winced.

"Don't be more of an idiot than you have to be. There's only one kind of employer who'd give you terms like that."

Boysie thought for a second. "Nefarious government job?"

"In one. Give the laddie a framed testimonial."

"No"

"Oh, Oakesie," Mostyn sighed. "We've done this scene a thousand times. Cut the rabbiting and come along. You'll give in eventually."

"What's the catch?"

"No catch."

"Field work? Death and destruction? People shooting at me?"

"Does a hundred quid a week sound like danger money?"

"Tax free it does. With that kind of crinkle I could afford to put down a deposit on a dirty weekend at the Hilton."

"You haven't any choice, Boysie, you're co-opted anyway. Just like your uncle Mostyn."

"Co-opted onto what?"

"SEAT."

"Stop arsing about, Mostyn."

"Special Executive for Anti-Terrorism."

"Then I do get shot at."

"Not in a million years. You sit on a committee. The job's good for a couple of years at least. The committee makes decisions on anti-terrorist activities-how to deal with bombings, hijackings, urban guerrilla warfare, airport shootouts and the like."

"Why me?" Reprise.

"You do have special knowledge."

"What special knowledge?"

"As I recall it, you did a number of clandestine operations for Special Security - correct me if I'm wrong, but you were our government-sponsored hit man, weren't you?"

Boysie's stomach performed a masterly series of tight turns. Mostyn knew very well that he had subcontracted a major percentage of the security killings with which he had been entrusted. All that had been revealed to the colonel during the Madrigal business.

"So?" he gulped.

"So you sit on the committee and give us the benefit of your knowledge." He dropped the key onto the floor. "Move in as soon as you like. Salary starts Monday. I'll be in touch over the weekend, the office is shrouded in mystery as always. Number 23 Pembridge Court, Shooter & Crump, Wholesale Toys. I've arranged for a hot and cold running redhead." Mostyn rose and walked, with his little prissy steps, towards the door. "Oh, and Boysie, there will be the odd jaunt: International Conferences and the like."

That was four weeks ago, and experience since then, had put Boysie's nerves on the brink. The flat was splendid: the money helped. He began to look more spruce and was able to fill some of the spaces in his record collection - Sinatra was being superseded by Stan Kenton, a fact probably of great significance to any passing shrink.

With the new cash-flow came women. Not in droves but at least in pairs and trios - a marked improvement, even though the hot and cold running redhead, to whom Mostyn had referred, turned out to be a henna-haired cleaning lady of indeterminate age.

It was the work which bothered Boysie. He did not mind the daily slog to Shooter & Crump Wholesale Toys, it was what happened there during the day that gave him a twitch. The whole thing tasted strongly of the Department and the old days. The ciphers and cut outs, odd couriers, the routine and scent of secrecy.

Boysie spent most of his time checking the Telex messages which, to be fair to Mostyn, were mainly *en clair*, dealt with wide security and terrorism and remained in the abstract, leaving Boysie personally uninvolved. Yet, in the background, between the Telex, the two secretaries, the nights out with Deborah Morton-Chambers and Anne Pilsbury-Worthley - who loved jazz and obscure foreign films respectively - Boysie was constantly nagged by a small and shrouded spectre in the back of his head. Something was up - high as a long-hung pheasant.

Then one morning a Telex arrived which he could neither decipher nor trace, apart from its Paris prefix. Mostyn smiled serenely when it was handed over.

"That's it, laddie. We're on our way."

Boysie felt the dormant nest of snakes uncoil in his nervous system. "On our way to where?"

"Conference. I warned you. International Conference in Paris." Mostyn's look doing credit to a jackal. "Go pack your case."

"We going to be away long?" Boysie swallowed. "Who can tell?" Mostyn spread his hands. "Just pack your case and don't leave out your pop gun."

The snakes writhed angrily. "I have to go heeled? Come on Mostyn, let me have the truth. It's the old old story, an operation, isn't it? Something's up."

"Not specially. But it is a conference on anti-terrorism and I'd hate us to get clobbered with no means of retaliation. Pack your iron." He patted Boysie's arm. "I'll feel that much safer. Travelling is dangerous these days."

Here he was then, packed and ready to go. He switched off the radio, plummeting Jimmy Young into oblivion, heaved on his coat and padded to the door. Leaving like this had an all too familiar feel about it, reminding him of the past. Leaving to be projected into danger. Danger was not Boysie's natural element.

He closed the door behind him with a lot of regret. After all he had been forced to cancel a crucial date with the lovely Anne Pilsbury-Worthley. Fornication had been high on the list of planned activities. More fish in the sea, he thought. Then, romantically, another time, another place: male chauvinist pig that he was.

III - REFRAIN

Words and music recurring at the end of each stanza

Mostyn was waiting at Heathrow, all done up in a dark brown suit covered by a long, fur-collared suede coat. Boysie thought he looked like an expensive rat.

As always, it was crowded and a lot of flights were late in getting off; the coffee tasted like superior sewage and all the young women, uniformed, stamping tickets, shepherding passengers and making announcements, had a self-satisfied, hygienic look: all margarine and Tampax, Boysie thought, clutching his duty-free cigarettes, sipping the deplorable coffee, and cocking an eye at the departures monitor.

Mostyn had little to say, his small eyes moving constantly over the changing sea of faces. Tourists had that glum look peculiar to their breed; bored lovers hunched over tables, not talking because they had said it all before and wanted nothing more than to be rid of one another. Outside the terminal the occasional sound of a jet winding down, or roaring off down a runway, made Boysie's stomach revolve with gentle regularity. He hated airports at the best of times, but international events - hijackings, terror attacks-had made it worse.

When their flight was eventually called they rose, in unison, still not conversing, flashing their magic plastic cards at passport control and waiting until the Special Branch man cleared them.

It was not until they were on board the Trident, with its engines growling, and some manic creature depositing dry ice in Boysie's veins, that Mostyn began any serious talk.

"Saw a friend of yours yesterday," he said, hardly moving his lips.

"Oh yes?" Boysie's voice sweeping unnaturally up the scale.

The tension was building, inseparable from his terror of flying. The additional fact that Mostyn had met an old friend merely compounded the fear. Two things engulfed Boysie's life - hysterical apprehension when flying and the consistent machinations of the wily little Mostyn.

The aircraft was taxiing up to the runway threshold and the combination of his two major horrors put Boysie's nervous system seriously on the blink: his mouth was filled with bile, palms oozed sweat, about sixty-four scaly creatures scuttled around in his stomach. Some of them appeared to be equipped with wings. Boysie shot an agonised glance towards his smirking chief. Mostyn seemed as relaxed as a bag of feathers.

Up on the flight deck, the captain called for full power, the engines leaped to a boiling whine, brakes came off and the Trident surged forward with all the accustomed thrust and judder.

Boysie closed his eyes and tried to concentrate on clearing his mind. Some people read books during take-off and landing. That would be a terrible way to go, thought Boysie: to be consumed in an aircraft disaster while reading Stanley Morgan.

The juddering ceased as the aircraft lifted and the familiar nausea rose. This was the dangerous moment. Or was it? Everything was a multiplication in danger when sitting next to James George Mostyn.

Boysie opened his eyes again.

"A friend of yours," repeated Mostyn, leaning casually towards the window. "Go uphill damned fast these things."

Boysie snapped down his lids again, blindly fumbling for the little paper bag they provided against throwing up.

Then the engines wound down to a gentle thrum. Looking around him, Boysie saw that the *Seatbelts/No Smoking* sign was off. People were lighting up and talking in the animated way they did when snatched from the edge of the grave.

"What friend?" Boysie struggled, trying to sound at ease.

"Charlie Griffin." Mostyn did not even smile.

"Oh Jesus," breathed Boysie.

Charlie Griffin of all people. Charlie Griffin, the undertaker to whom he had subcontracted a large proportion of the deadly assignments in the days with the Department. Mostyn knew all about Charlie Griffin and he would not mention him unless there was cause. Mostyn, devious little bugger that he was: devious Svengali whose psychological hold over Boysie was so inexplicable that it even frightened him to think about it. It was from Mostyn that all good things flowed, and all bad.

"There's something bloody on," said Boysie. A flat and tired statement.

"Can't think what you mean." Mostyn beckoned to a passing hostess. "Two large whiskies, my dear."

The girl nodded, and Boysie was flattered to see that her gaze rested on him rather than the oily Mostyn. We could render him down, Boysie thought. Render the little devil down and the result would go a long way to solving the power shortage. There was enough oil in Mostyn to light London for a month or two.

"Of course you bloody know what I mean. You think I'm a cretin? Don't answer that. You've done it again you evil little bastard. Whip in Oakes, he's the perfect idiot fall-guy. What are you, Mostyn, the Marquis de Sade or something?"

"Or something. I bumped into Charlie Griffin quite by chance. By accident. He was with a dark young woman with obviously over-active glands."

"Freud maintained there are no such things as accidents." Boysie had heard the remark on a TV chat show and cherished it ever since.

Mostyn gave him a quick look of reappraisal and the hostess arrived with the drinks. As she leaned over to serve Mostyn, her right breast lightly brushed Boysie's left cheek. He automatically raised a hand. The sap rose and spring blossomed in the aircraft cabin.

"Down, Oakesie," muttered Mostyn. "She works for us." There was a long pause.

"That's a coincidence." Boysie bit out the words. "I work for you as well. You've done it again, haven't you? There's something on."

Mostyn gave him an unctuous smile. "Nothing much. But there's always safety in numbers. She'll be joining us in Paris and, old Oakes, I want none of the familiar."

There was the usual ten minutes hell as they made their let-down and final approach to Paris, Charles De Gaulle. During the approach, Boysie tried to be objective about himself, but all he saw was a big tough-looking man with fading good looks and the knowledge that inside that steely exterior there was a persistent mass of jellified cowardice. It sickened him.

They touched down, the engines howling in reverse thrust, the aircraft slowing to a steady roll. Boysie breathed freely, savouring the feeling of intense relief and mentally kissing mother earth.

"Now that we're down will you tell me about it?"

"As far as you're concerned we're here for the SEAT International Conference," chanted Mostyn smugly.

The hostess was standing by the exit as they deplaned: five-ten, dark hair, large brown eyes, a figure not only built for glory but also lavishly tended, and a face which reflected vulnerability, helplessness and sexual promise in equal proportions. Boysie knew about girls whose faces reflected vulnerability, helplessness and sexual promise. They were usually quite capable of looking after themselves, thank you very much. They were also apt to kick you in the crotch.

"Goodbye, sir, hope we see you again," said the hostess, metaphorically kicking Boysie in the crotch.

"Yes, ma'am," he grinned. "Yes, ma'am, indeed."

The car which awaited them had a uniformed chauffeur who looked not unlike Sean Connery. The car looked like a souped-up Mercedes, and there was another fellow tagging along - big, with muscles like great lumps of iron. A heavy, Boysie rightly deduced.

Mostyn waved a hand, flapping back and forth between the heavy and Boysie.

"Boysie Oakes, this is Gerard Couperose. Sûreté Nationale."

The two men looked at each other like wrestlers before a bout.

"Department of Intelligence?" Boysie questioned. Couperose gave a small, friendly, nod and extended a massive hand.

"Enchanté Monsieur Oakes. The Colonel has told me much about you."

They locked hands. For a moment it appeared to be a trial of strength.

"Gerard is attached on this trip," Mostyn cut in. "Liaison and all that."

"All that," repeated Boysie with a tone meant to convey significance, reflecting upon how much he had learned over the years. He knew about girls like the one on the aircraft; he also knew about men like Gerard Couperose from the Sûreté's Department of Intelligence. They were, like the girls, prone to kicking one in the crotch.

Aloud he said, "Why did I ever fall for it?"

"Fall for what?" Mostyn, spry from the rear of the Merc.

Boysie got in, slumping next to the dapper little Colonel. "For whatever you're going to do to me," he answered. "Or for whatever you're going to make me do. For all the pain and bloody danger you're going to expose me to."

"To which we're going to expose you," corrected Mostyn, punctuating the sentence with a smile: a blizzard of some proportions.

The Merc set off smoothly with Couperose sitting next to the driver.

"Mademoiselle Lyric is here?" he asked, twisting to look back at Mostyn. They were obviously old buddies. "She'll join us at the Baltimore."

"Lyric?" snorted Boysie. "What sort of a name is Lyric?"

"The name of the young woman whose tit you were touching up on the aircraft."

"Oh her. One of ours, you said. Spies and secrets. I thought that kind of skulduggery went out years ago."

"Yes, one of ours; and, no, it didn't go out years ago."

"I didn't touch her up, but you couldn't blame me if I did: it's about the only genuine human pastime left. Everything else is electronics and computers. Even the secret world is remote-controlled - no secrets, not ones kept by humans anyway; it's all memory banks and tapes that wipe if they're opened the wrong way, self-destruct mechanisms; there's nothing individual anymore."

"You are jaded, Monsieur Oakes, yes?" Couperose fixed him with a look of stressed steel.

"I am jaded," agreed Boysie sadly. "Bloody jaded. What gives with the Lyric bird?"

"Lyric Lavenham." Mostyn savoured the name.

"Sounds like someone from Dornford Yates."

Couperose looked puzzled. "What is Dornford Yates?" "I might have known a Frenchman wouldn't have heard of Dornford Yates. Besides, you'd be too young to remember him. He was a writer of fiction, Gerard mon vieux." Boysie bitter. "He did what they used to call adventure yarns. Telephones ringing in Surrey mansions. Night drives across Europe. Mysterious schlosses in pine forests, where the heroes meet the gross villains; and there were splendid heroines who never screwed and had small feet. Gave me quite a foot fetish, Dornford Yates."

Couperose raised his eyes to heaven. "*Fou*," he said quietly.

They were in heavy traffic, moving, in the middle lane, at around seventy.

"You're becoming boring, Boysie," sighed Mostyn.

"And what about Monsieur Griffin?" Couperose asked the Colonel.

"I knew it," murmured Boysie. "Bloody knew it. Hoist with your own petard, Mostyn you bastard."

"Shut up." Sharp from Mostyn.

"I bumped into Charlie Griffin quite by chance," chuntered Boysie. "By accident. He was with a dark girl with over-active glands."

"I like Monsieur Griffin," Couperose smiled. "So droll."

"He's about as droll as a bloody hearse."

"We're being followed," Mostyn said suddenly. "White Peugeot two cars behind. Three men. They pulled out of the airport just after us: been leeching it all the way. Could have taken us a dozen times but they're deliberately holding back."

"Jesus," said Boysie.

Couperose was speaking rapidly to the driver. "I've told Charlot to test it," he turned, looking back along the road.

Boysie had been right about the Merc, it was souped-up. Charlot, the driver, had extended his arms like a racing driver.

"He know his stuff?" Mostyn asked quietly.

Couperose nodded as the Merc swept forward, dancing to the left and picking up speed like an executive jet.

"Jesus," said Boysie again as Charlot weaved the car through traffic with the speedo needle flicking into the high figures. The winged and scaly creatures were performing an intricate ballet in his guts again.

"Limpet." Mostyn terse, his eyes on their rear. "They're further back but shortening distance."

Couperose was talking into a transceiver. "The man himself?" he asked.

"Not a chance."

"What man?" Boysie knew he was showing signs of personal fear.

"There they go, dropping back. You can tell Charlot to ease off."

"What man?" asked Boysie.

"Just a marker?" queried Couperose.

"What man?" asked Boysie.

"Straightforward," Mostyn answered Couperose. "A check to make sure we're going where they think we're going."

"It makes sense."

"What bleeding man?" Boysie shouted.

"Not yet," Mostyn answered quietly.

"Why not yet?"

"All in good time."

"Why not yet? For Chrissake I know I've been conned into something, so what man and why not yet?"

"All in good time. When we meet Lyric at the hotel."

"And Griffin?" There was considerable frustration and menace in his voice.

The pause was punctuated by a voice chattering French police matters on Couperose's transceiver.

Mostyn nodded. "And Griffin."

"Not even a clue?" Boysie wheedled. "A small hint?"

Mostyn smiled. There were fangs in there somewhere, thought Boysie.

"Thirty-two across," smarmed Mostyn, his voice cooing.

"What do you hit under pressure?"

Pressure was the code word they had used in the Department when a kill was imminent. Cloak and dagger again.

"Target," said Boysie, sounding as though he had found the lost chord.

"Good. That's your clue and the answer."

"Oh no." It was Boysie's turn to smile. "No, Mostyn. I'm not hitting any more targets: not for you, the Prime Minister, the Leader of the Opposition, the Chiefs-of-Staff or even the Lord Privy Seal himself."

"Nobody's asking you." Mostyn grinned. It was a horrible sight. "Somebody else is under Pressure. You're the Target. You and me both."

"Turn around. I want out."

"Too late. It wouldn't make much difference now. We've been set-up, old lad, and we want to catch the beggar at it."

Boysie felt sick, the waves of nausea and depression building like a sudden bore through the estuary of his nervous system.

IV - DIRGE

A lament usually connected with funerals

To find the Hotel Baltimore, you dodge around the Place Charles De Gaulle and drive about a quarter of a mile up the broad Avenue Kleber. The hotel is tucked away in a side street on the right: a nice little family hotel, not luxurious, but not entirely inexpensive either.

A uniformed commissionaire trotted out and relieved them of their luggage as soon as the Merc drew up in front of the facade.

Boysie climbed out, trying desperately to sublimate his fears by working at being nonchalant. He sniffed the air like a hound trying to pick up the scent. Paris had a special smell which Boysie always associated with sex. But then he associated most pleasant smells with sex. Here it was exhaust fumes overlaid by Gauloise, coffee and the aroma of svelte ladies.

"Paris," sighed Boysie. "Paris always affects me like this, Mostyn. Makes me bloody randy."

Inside, Boysie was still in near panic. It was funny, he thought, how fear always turned him on to sex. Someone once said it was a desire to escape back into the darkness of the womb.

"You'll really have to control the hornier-than-thou-attitude, Oakes," snapped Mostyn. "It's unbecoming, and, besides, I will not have that kind of trouble on this operation."

"It was a straightforward business trip - a Conference - when we started out," Boysie was edging towards the main doors and natural cover. "Now it's an operation." Their accommodation was on the fifth floor and Mostyn called a meeting for half-an-hour after their arrival.

In room 540, Boysie found that he had been provided with a large bed, heavy old-fashioned wardrobe and dressing table, and a bathroom which seemed to be a junction for every water pipe in the building.

Out of habit from the old days, Boysie automatically checked the place for bugs - light fittings, the headboard of the bed, under the bedside lamps and table. He found nothing so carried on with the unpacking, laid out an impressive array of men's toiletries on the glass shelf above the washbasin, freshened up, cast a professional eye out of the window to see if the room was overlooked by anywhere which could provide a good aiming point for a sniper, decided that there were three possibilities, left hurriedly and made his way to 542, which was Mostyn's lair.

The two windows in Mostyn's room faced a brick wall and were not overlooked by would-be firing points. It was also a larger room than Boysie's and, when he entered, two other people were there besides Mostyn and the Frenchman, Couperose. Lyric Lavenham, now wearing brown boots and a simple brown cord dress with brass buttons, relaxed calmly in an armchair. She was showing a great deal of highly speculative thigh, and brightened visibly when Boysie entered.

"Hallo, Mr. Oakes, nice to see you," grinned Griffin from one of the other chairs. Even though he could be aptly described as grey and nondescript, there was no mistaking Griffin - thin, ferrety and horn-rimmed.

"I heard you were coming," Boysie threw at him, advancing on the glowing Miss Lavenham. "Hallo, we didn't get properly introduced on the plane. My name's Oakes. Boysie Oakes."

"Hallo," all throaty. "I know who you are, I've been looking forward to this."

"Perhaps we can get on," a weary monotone from Mostyn. "I have to conduct a briefing."

"Yeees," Boysie irretrievably distracted.

"Well, sit down."

Boysie looked around him abstractedly, finally found a chair, at the end of the room furthest from the lovely Miss Lavenham, shrugged and moved towards it.

"Drinking, Mr Oakes? It's a long time since we had a snort together." Griffin grinned. He was now standing by a well-stocked drinks trolley. The unclassifiable Griffin always surprised Boysie with his paradoxical subservience laced with social confidence.

Boysie accepted a large Scotch. "You're offensively friendly, Charles," he tipped his glass towards the undertaker. "Business brisk, is it?"

"Can't grumble," Griffin returned to his seat.

“If you’ve finished with the small talk.” Mostyn was perched on the corner of the table, beady eyes glittering, his tone that of a sarcastic schoolmaster.

“I finished a long time ago,” Boysie held his gaze. “I’d like to make that quite clear.”

Mostyn switched his smile on and off. “Clarity begins at home.” He thought himself no end of a wag.

Lyric caught Boysie’s eye. They looked at each other, deadpan.

“Well, if we’re all set, I’ll start.” Mostyn began.

“Oakes here said something quite perceptive when we were coming in from the airport. He said there were no secrets kept by humans anymore: that it’s all done by electronics and computers nowadays. To some extent he’s right. The trade most of us remember - the plotting and counterplotting, the game of truth or dare - has changed.”

“Lyric’s not old enough to remember that kind of game,” Boysie tried, courteously.

“She’s read the right books,” snapped Mostyn. “What I’m getting at is that, in the hard light of day, most of us are redundant.”

“Like ledger clerks and travel agents-real travel agents, not package procurers.” Boysie sounded acid.

“Like a lot of things,” Mostyn actually appeared to be showing signs of friendly agreement. “Like real vegetables, unfrozen, straight out of the ground; like some of the ideals many of us had.”

“Is this getting us anywhere?” Boysie sipped his drink. He spoke very quietly so that only Mostyn and Griffin picked up the words.

Mostyn looked at him, unblinking. “The ideals, the reasons, the methods have all changed. Soon you’ll be asked, what did you do in the Cold War, daddy?”

Boysie was equally unblinking. “I killed people who were a risk to national security.”

“Except when I did it for you.” Griffin mouthed, forming the words with his lips but letting no sound escape. He looked as solemn as one of his corpses.

“It’s about the only thing that hasn’t changed,” Mostyn nodded. “Humans still kill to protect and defend. They also kill for revenge.” His hand slid into his breast pocket taking out a little stack of what looked like picture postcards. "I wonder if you remember any of these faces, Boysie."

He began to deal the cards onto the table in a line. They were photographs of people. Seven in all. Six men and a woman.

Boysie shifted to get a better view. "Christ," he said. "That's old Martin, I'd almost forgotten about him."

Mostyn nodded again. "Any of the others?"

"Martin. Nick Holborn. Is that Grenot?"

Couperose craned forward. "Jean-Paul Grenot, yes. I knew him well. I worked with him."

"*Knew* him?"

"Last year." Mostyn tensing. "He bought it."

"I hadn't heard. I'm sorry, he was a nice guy."

"No reason for you to have heard. Any of the others?"

"The girl, of course."

"Of course. Name? Or can't you recall unless the photograph is full-length and nude?"

"Her name's Palmer. Jean, no Joan. Joan Palmer."

"Good."

"And Goldfinch, Herbie Goldfinch."

"I recognise him." Griffin was joining in.

"Mike something, that one," Boysie's finger stabbing.

"An American, Mike Smith."

"Yes."

"The last one's my brother." Lyric had come over and was standing behind Mostyn.

"Bob Lavenham," crowed Boysie. "Geez is Bob Lavenham your brother? I remember Bob Lavenham." He stopped short looking at Lyric's face.

"*Was* her brother, Boysie." Mostyn's voice low, like a funereal vicar.

"I'm sorry, Lyric. I ..."

"Didn't know? Why should you?" The girl gave him a shy, sad look.

"They've all gone," said Mostyn, matter-of-fact.

"Gone?"

"Chopped."

"What, Martin and Joan Palmer and ...?"

"Herbie Goldfinch?" Griffin actually looked shocked.

"The lot. All of them. Part of our past; of the rare days."

"All seven?" Boysie sounded as though he did not really believe it.

"I've told you. Can you now understand why we're all here - bearing in mind that Gerard was Jean-Paul Grenot's junior assistant in the mid-sixties?"

Boysie's mind tumbled down through the past. There were a lot of names, faces, times and places which were jumbled at this distance. Martin, for instance, had been the Department's man at Heathrow for a long time; he had also been with Mostyn during the business in Switzerland: the Amber Nine business. Boysie did not care to think of Martin as a corpse. He centred his mind on the three photographs which were out of key - the Palmer girl, Grenot, and the American, Mike Smith.

He recalled Joan Palmer as being one of the least exotic people in the Department. Tall and rather angular, but, like so many birds who did not exude natural sensuality, she had been a cracker when the chips were down. He had a mental picture of her in some hotel bedroom, late at night – naturally - and only partially clad. She had been some lay, male chauvinist pig that he was, though he did not remember that she had complained.

Where in hell was that hotel? There were two paintings to the left of the bed, red, gold and black, picking out the decor of the room. Plush, very plush. Big heavy lamps. Gold-flecked wallpaper. Flash, it was coming back. He had fallen asleep after they had ... well, after.

"It's time you were getting ready, Boysie. Time to go." That was when he examined the wallpaper, yawning and rubbing his eyes, coming awake.

"Coffee, Boysie. You've got time for coffee. It's ..."

It's what? Five o'clock? Half-past? That was it, she was his alarm clock. Mostyn admitted it afterwards. He knew Boysie could never resist one of the girls from the Department, and Joan Palmer had been a set-up to make sure he was awake and off in time. But where the hell was it?

"Puebla," he said aloud. "The Mexican thing. Pinkney. Pinkney and Defoe. Nineteen sixty ..."

"Sixty-four." Mostyn nodded.

"I was on that." Griffin smirked.

"We didn't know it at the time, though, Charles. We didn't even know you were in town." Mostyn tapped a cigarette against a slim case which could have been made of platinum. “You were a very clever boy, Boysie, because we should have known about Charles. There were enough of us around.”

But Boysie didn’t hear him, his thoughts, and senses, were back in ‘64, in Mexico, sitting in the big Lincoln convertible with Mostyn, the American, Smith, and Jean-Paul Grenot, sweeping down the super-highway from Mexico City and praying that Griffin had got into Puebla before them.

V - ROMANCERO

Song describing the deeds of heroes

Boysie was lying on his bed, in the flat off Chesham Place, on a Thursday afternoon in late June, 1964, when he got the Pressure warning. The girl lying on the bed with him was a black lady of irresistible proportions, called Vita.

The telephone rang. Boysie groaned, disentangled himself from the coffee-cream thighs and arms, stretched out and grunted into the receiver.

"Mostyn," snarled Mostyn at the other end.

"Yes?" Wary.

"Pressure, laddie. I want to talk to you about this one. It's a combined op, lots of detail, and I'll be coming with you."

Insects crawled itchily up the back of his neck. "When?" he asked, throwing a nervous look in Vita's direction.

"If you can spare the time, in about half-an-hour."

"Well."

"Sorry to interrupt anything if you're having a chummy time, lad, but we *do* pay you,"

"Yes, yes, of course." He swallowed, the saliva thickening in his throat, the left side of his mouth twitching. "Of course, I'll be right over."

"You'll be right over what, honey?" breathed Vita, rubbing his thigh enthusiastically.

"Work, baby," Boysie looked at her ruefully as he replaced the receiver.

Vita groaned. "So you're sending me back to the jungle, just like that, uhu?"

"No other way. In any case, your jungle has all modern conveniences including head hunters. I've been there. Remember?"

She sighed, moving from the bed. The way she stretched, arching her body, brought on further frustration for Boysie, so that he was forced to turn away as she began to pull on her clothes.

He showered, saw Vita off the premises, dressed and put in a quick call to Griffin.

"Nice to hear your voice, Mr. Oakes. We in business again?"

"I think so, Mr. Griffin. I'll give you the details within twenty-four hours."

"Always happy to oblige a regular customer. I'll place myself on alert so to speak."

Boysie trotted downstairs, climbed into his E-Type Jag - these were the days before he took to sporting a Jensen - and gunned off in the direction of Whitehall and the building which served as a front for the Department of Special Security.

He crossed the unimposing foyer - decorated in an overall shade of Opposition Vomit - entered the lift, permanently marked OUT OF ORDER, slipped his key into the door at the back of the lift and went into the reception area.

A girl, looking as though she had been culled from the pages of *Vogue*, was on duty.

"Number Two's waiting for you in his office," she smiled cheerfully, yet in a way suggesting that, in some previous existence she had been Marie Antoinette, and Boysie was one of the masses whom she had instructed should eat cake if they did not have bread.

Marie Antoinette signed him in, noting the time from a Cartier watch which would not have left much change from a five-hundred-pound cheque, and nodded him away as though her head was weighed down by her false eyelashes. One day, Boysie thought, the lashes would fall off and join all the others in that great beauty salon in the sky.

He went over to the main lift and pressed the button for the third floor where Mostyn had his office. In the third-floor corridor a Department watchdog sat cleaning his fingernails like a hood in some old B movie - life imitating sub-art. Boysie swallowed and tapped on Mostyn's door.

Mostyn stood at his window looking down onto the filtering traffic below.

He turned, as Boysie came into the room, took an exaggerated look at his Rolex Oyster, dropped his eyes to examine the high-gloss polish on the immaculate shoes, finally shifting his gaze across the carpet to Boysie's feet.

"Trouble with the car?" he asked, eyes narrowing and the head waggling arrogantly.

"No." Boysie refused the sarcastic hurdle.

"Never mind. Sit down, old lad, and I will to thee a tale unfold."

"You said it was Pressure."

"It is Pressure, but you can't be on your own."

"I'm not happy about that."

Indeed he was not. The last thing Boysie needed was other people in the Department weaving around the target area. They might see far too much.

"It's not a question of what you like, it's a matter of circumstances. There're two targets, one of ours and a Frog. We've got a lot of people near them already, including Frog security and the CIA, both of whom want them intact."

"And we don't?"

"Many heads will drop into the basket if these two jokers return." Mostyn contrived a sinister voice.

"Okay. Names and addresses."

Boysie always made a show of great professionalism at this point of a Pressure alert. It helped, he felt, to instil confidence. It also gave him maximum information as quickly as possible, which was a help for getting Griffin organised.

"I told you it's not easy," the Colonel took out his key chain unlocking a desk drawer, dropping two folders onto the leather in front of his tame executioner.

"Names: Pinkney, Norman Arthur; and Defoe, Paul."

Boysie looked at the two photographs. The men seemed to be roughly the same age - early forties. Pinkney was dark, square featured, Germanic; Defoe slim-faced, aesthetic features, light sandy hair.

"Addresses?"

"There's the rub. They've faded. They're both in Mexico."

Boysie's heart skipped, his guts filling with bubbling liquid in which small sharks swam aggressively. Mexico would not, he thought, be happy news for Griffin.

"Mexico?" he quavered.

" 'Fraid so. South of the border and all that."

"Where in Mexico?"

"Mexico City yesterday, but they've moved on now."

"Moved on where, for crying out loud?"

"Don't worry, dear boy. We won't lose them. I've got a four-man tail on them."

"Interchangeable, I hope."

Some of Mostyn's people were as casual as labourers in a minefield.

"Of course. Four of the brightest boys in the business."

"They'd better be."

"Old Martin, you get on with Martin; and Bob Lavenham, Herbie Goldfinch, Nick Holborn."

"Good lads, why in hell can't they ...?"

"Because we pay you to do it and no questions."

"The problem is that I'm being Pressured as well."

"Ah."

"CIA'd like my guts on the ancestral silverware, and the Sûreté's Department of Intelligence are muttering things not unconnected with Dr. Guillotine's unpleasant little invention."

Boysie had a pleasing mental picture of Mostyn making a brave speech from the tumbril while sock-knitting crones of grim visage made cackling noises. The camera of his mind moved up the steps of the scaffold and into Big Close-Up of the Executioner. It was himself, clad in body-moulded tights and a smile.

"Where do you think they are now?"

"I haven't the faintest idea. It doesn't matter though."

"It matters to me."

Mostyn's smile greased across his face. "But I shall be with you, old Oakes. Like a guardian angel."

Boysie remained silent, the thought of Mostyn as a guardian angel would still the tongues of even the heavenly choir.

"I'll lead you to them," said Mostyn as if he was performing a great service. "Then I call off the markers and unleash you."

"I would prefer to know exactly ..."

"Why?"

"I just like to be prepared. The kind of clothes I should take and all that sort of thing."

"It's not a brewers' outing, lad; not a merry mystery tour."

"No, it's one of your business trips, and I know your business trips. I've got an image to keep ..."

"In case you hadn't heard, the cult of the individual is not encouraged these days. Just pack a couple of lightweight suits and some woollies for the cold nights." With his fingertips, Mostyn slid the photographs of the targets across the desk. He followed up with a little cardboard wallet. "Airline tickets. Money. I go this afternoon. You leave Heathrow tonight. Economy class."

Boysie scratched his head, looking down on the pictures of the two doomed men.

"Can I be told why they have to be ...?"

"Just take it from me that they're very hot gentlemen. They have to be wasted." The nasty smile had disappeared.

"One of ours, and a Frog," Boysie mused. "Will the opposition be active?"

"As beavers. The Americans and French are running interference, and you can be certain the others'll be making it difficult."

"I have to be told more than that. I have to know ..."

Mostyn rose, irritation crossing his face like a thunder-cloud. Then he hesitated and lowered his rump into the chair again.

"All right. It won't mean anything, but Pinkney and Defoe were working on something called Project Clambake."

"Joint Op?"

"NATO," Mostyn nodded. "Paris based."

"And they've skipped with the microfilm and the plans?"

"You've been seeing too many spy movies. There is no microfilm." He tapped his forehead. "It's all in there: in their crafty little noddles. French Intelligence rumbled them a couple of weeks ago. Our people went over and they've all been hanging around, gorging themselves on government expenses, waiting for the two lads to run Eastwards, and tripping over each other's feet." He gave a dry laugh. "They even know the contact, a greaseball freelance called Caesar Chiliman. When they ran ..."

"They didn't go East."

"Of course not. We could've told 'em that. While everyone was out-thinking everyone else, they got on a plane to South America. Luckily I anticipated them. That's how we got a fix on them in Mexico City."

"Where they aren't anymore."

"Precisely. There are several objectives, depending on where you happen to be standing. The French and Americans want to whip 'em in."

"And we want to close them."

Mostyn looked at him, hard, the eyes brilliant. "Then there's friend Chiliman."

"Who wants them to make their drop."

"If you can call it a drop. We haven't heard from him, but Chiliman is almost certainly selling them to the highest bidder; and whoever buys needs the bodies intact, alive and well, ready to sing cadenzas. You can bet your pension that, wherever Pinkney and Defoe are, Chiliman will not be far behind."

"With heavies?"

"Grossly overburdened with heavies, I should imagine. Once we've marked 'em, Boysie boy, and drawn off the Frogs and Yanks, you'll have to get in there quick. No messing, and none of your subtle accidents. All I want is a couple of bodies, very much filtered from life." The small colonel sighed. "That's it then. You don't need to know any more."

"Not even Clambake?"

"Especially not even Clambake."

Boysie's head swarmed with panicky bees, while the anxiety butterflies used his stomach wall as a skating rink.

"Mexico then," he said with resignation. "I'll go and pack."

"You'll be met in Mexico City. See you there."

Boysie was almost at the door when he heard the heavy metallic thud on Mostyn's desk, followed by two lighter thumps.

"Don't forget this, Boysie. You just might need it."

The thud came from the big wicked Colt automatic, the two smaller noises from the spare pair of magazines.

Boysie looked at the weapon with disgust. The room seemed suddenly to be oppressively hot, and the weapon huge on the desk. He could use a Colt forty-five : no problem; in fact he could use it very well, but that did not mean he had to like the thing, or, for that matter, use it in cold blood.

"How to make friends and influence people," Boysie said flatly.

"How to keep friends and people of influence." Mostyn turned away, as though he did not want to see his underling pluck the gun from the desk.

Back in Chesham Place, Boysie slurped a generous amount of brandy into a balloon glass and started to pack. All the time his mind grappled with the problem of Griffin. The terror inside concerned the possibility of actually having to dispatch Pinkney and Defoe. Griffin was the only person who could take the weight of that responsibility from his shoulders. But there were difficulties-how would Griffin feel about Mexico? If he agreed, how could Boysie finger the targets and maintain contact?

In the end, he decided there was nothing for it but a direct confrontation.

They met in what was then the Lyons' Corner House in Coventry Street, Boysie's pockets bulging with the photographs of Pinkney and Defoe, together with five hundred pounds mad money which he always kept for emergencies.

Griffin had arrived first and procured a table for two in the crowded downstairs tearoom, his thin lugubrious face wreathed in a toothy smile, eyes restless behind the horn-rimmed glasses.

"Hope you like ham and tomato, Mr. Oakes. I took the liberty of ordering."

"Just a cup of tea, please." Boysie sank into the chair opposite this nondescript, deadly man.

"Sticky cake? Meringue?"

"Just the tea."

"They're very good."

"Mr. Griffin, please, just the tea, it's been a long day."

"Should keep up your strength, Mr. Oakes. You look as if you've got a problem." Griffin was an extraordinary blend ruthlessness and concern mingling in unequal proportions. "One or two?"

"One or two what?"

"Lumps, Mr. Oakes."

"Oh. Two."

" 'Scuse fingers. I've been laying out a poor old dear in Chelsea, took sudden by a number forty-six bus. But I scrubbed me hands well before coming here."

Boysie blanched visibly and swallowed hard.

Griffin passed over the tea, grinned and leaned back, his hand hovering over the plate of sandwiches.

"Now, Mr. Oakes. Who's it to be this time?"

"There're two." Boysie dropped his voice.

"Double event," said Griffin loudly. "The more the merrier. Don't look so perturbed, Mr. Oakes, you and I've been doing business long enough now. How do you fancy them going? We haven't had a good lift shaft job lately, that might be nice. As I recall it, the lady we did last month went by way of her domestic electricity supply. Neat and tasteful, I thought. You were pleased with that?"

"Yes, very pleased."

Boysie was jumpy. It had been a lady filing clerk at the Ministry of Defence in a highly sensitive situation with an unpleasant operative from one of the Eastern embassies.

"What for these two then? Lift shaft? Accidental explosion? Hit and run? The old six-storey drop? Carbon monoxide? The arsenical chocs? You name it, Mr. Oakes."

"Mr. Griffin," Boysie plunged. "We have a problem."

"Your credit's good with me, Mr. Oakes."

"No, it's not that."

"Well, problems are meant to be overcome, as my old Mum used to say."

"Our two friends - they're men, by the way - are ... well, they're touring."

Griffin flashed his nicotine-stained teeth again. "That shouldn't be much of a bother. Where're they touring then, Lake District? Oh, I hope it's the Lake District. Remember once I attended a most interesting gypsy funeral in the Lake District. Burning the caravan, the lot. Most rewarding."

Boysie shook his head. "It's not the Lake District. Would you believe, Mexico?"

"Mexico, yes, well ..." The full significance did not penetrate for a second. "Mexico?" he eventually shouted.

"Please, Mr. Griffin, keep your voice down."

"Mr. Oakes, I hope you're not being funny. Mexico's a long way off."

"Out of sight," said Boysie aloud. He felt furtive, the way he was watching Griffin's face, eyes and hands for a sign.

"I mean I do have my business to think of," continued Griffin hardly pausing. "I've got a cremation on Saturday and it's that bloody curate from St. Mark's: I can't leave him on his own. Last time he did one, he pressed the button and confined the deceased to the flames before the mourners even got into the chapel. Most distressing. They all expected to make their farewells to Aunt Rosie, and, pouf, she was gone before they knew it. A case of ashes to ashes prematurely. His mind was elsewhere, he said; and I know where it was, Mr. Oakes, on that blonde Sunday School teacher they got there. I don't know what's happening to the gentlemen of the cloth these days."

"It'll pay well," tried Boysie.

"I don't know as how that's the point, Mr. Oakes."

"They do say that Mexico's an interesting country."

"Yes, I'm sure: all that mañana and Chili con Carne.

Plays havoc with the digestion, but I couldn't get there and back before Saturday, could I? What sort of money?"

The trump. "Twice the usual and all expenses."

Griffin contemplated his bitten sandwich.

"Whereabouts in Mexico?"

"Well, Mexico City first. I've got the name of a good hotel. If you book in there, I could get a message to you. All you'd have to do is get there and I'd pass on the instructions."

"Complicated." Griffin popped the remainder of the sandwich into his mouth, chewed and selected another. "I have to admit that Mexico's a bit of a challenge. I mean there would probably be a lot of interesting variations. You could improvise in Mexico: Chili con Carne a shade too hot, or the tequila more toxic."

"I don't think this would be one for refinements, Mr. Griffin. It calls for speed."

"Ah," Griffin nodded sagely. "An in and out job. I warm to Mexico, Mr. Oakes. When would I be required to leave."

"Tonight. We'd travel separately, of course, but on the same flight." There was a deep gut reaction as the horrible truth drilled its way into his mind. Flying tonight. Off we go into the wide sky yonder. Jesus, he almost upchucked at the thought.

Griffin appeared to be preoccupied with his choice of cake. The meringue made it by a short head from the strawberry tartlet.

"Right, Mr. Oakes, you're on. Just point me in the general direction and I'll try to give satisfaction for money."

VI - ZARZUELA

Musical entertainment with spoken dialogue, often satirical

The Air France Flight 707 - ex-Paris, ex-New York - let down its gear, turned onto the final heading and slid down through the clear air towards Mexico City's Central Airport. It was now Friday evening; nearly nine o'clock local time.

Boysie was tired, crumpled, sweaty and undeniably scruffy, having not fully appreciated that his flight out of Heathrow, on the Thursday evening, called for a fifteen-hour wait in Paris before boarding the direct flight to South America - if an hour and half turn-round at New York could be classed as direct.

He closed his eyes, speculating on impending disaster, as the four Pratt & Whitney turbo-fans settled into their throttled-back whine on final approach.

They touched down with hardly a judder. Boysie opened his eyes, then quickly closed them again as the reverse-thrust filled the cabin. Queasy, he thought to himself, that is what flying makes you, queasy and scared shitless into the bargain.

He was the third person off the aircraft, stepping gingerly and savouring each time the soles of his shoes made contact with friendly mother earth. In the back of his head the soundtracks of a hundred B movies, all set in Mexico, amalgamated into a throbbing of guitars and wail of clarinets. Zorro, Cisco and Zapata had passed this way. Now El Oakes stepped into the arena.

He was pulled from the warm fantasy by an official, with several tons of gold in his mouth, asking for his passport. The customs and immigration business was relatively painless, the wheels having undoubtedly been already oiled well with pesos.

Passport stamped and the Revelation suitcase marked, Boysie ambled into the main concourse, blinking, looking around for his contact, and fending off cab drivers who propositioned him with a kind of frustrated indifference. He controlled his urge to look back among the other passengers emerging from the control points. Griffin would be with them, bound, as soon as possible, for the Bamer Hotel.

The Bamer was a luxury caravanserai and Boysie would be picking up the tab. He resented this, but in the tricky game they played it was essential that Griffin was kept happy; and Griffin was always happy when someone embalmed him in a cocoon of fleshly cosseting.

"Thou shalt not kill." The words came from a smiling, tanned and blond young man: tall, slim, and looking as though violence would never enter his head.

Boysie struggled to recall the code exchange, given to him on the telephone by the duty officer just before leaving London.

"Thou shalt not kill," repeated the contact.

"But need'st not strive: officiously to keep alive," Boysie parroted. It was one of Mostyn's little jokes.

The young man stuck out a big hand. "Lavenham," he grinned. "Bob Lavenham."

"Oakes," said Boysie, somewhat formally. "Boysie Oakes."

"Yes. Number Two told me to see you into your hotel - our hotel: everyone's there."

Boysie wondered who "everyone" was. "Lead me to it."

He hoped it was not the Bamer. Griffin could always be too close for comfort.

Outside, among the departing cabs and private cars, all of which seemed to be rehearsing for Le Mans, stood a shining ridiculously clean Lincoln Convertible. At the wheel was a small, ginger-haired man with bright eyes and an ominous bulge in his jacket.

Lavenham opened the rear door and motioned Boysie inside, following quickly. The ginger-haired one gunned the car fast from the kerb and joined the race.

"Glad to have you on the team. I'm Herbie Goldfinch." Boysie flinched as the driver turned round to squint at him.

"Hi," said Boysie with little enthusiasm. These two were the first, and they were here in Mexico City; there were more at the hotel and, doubtless, others still tailing Pinkney and Defoe. Half the population appeared to be members of the Department. "Which hotel?" he asked.

"Plush," smiled Lavenham. "*Tiene today las i comodi-dades modernas*."

“All mod cons,” translated Goldfinch. “Including a very fanciable chambermaid called Juanita.”

“Keep your lecherous hands on the wheel, Herbie.” Lavenham seemed to smile eternally. “We’re at The Alameda.”

Boysie tried to remember where The Alameda was. He had done a little homework on the aircraft: studying the street plan. From memory The Alameda was not far from the Bamer, a fact which might make life a little easier.

From the smooth interior of the car, Mexico City looked superbly interesting, a tangled shuffling of an old culture with the new-neon, glass and concrete at odds with baroque and the older Aztec influences.

They negotiated the heavy traffic through the Zocalo, passing the Cathedral gleaming under its floodlights, then on along the Avenue Juarez with the Alameda Park on their right.

As he thought, the Alameda was almost next door to the Bamer, which could make matters easier - or harder depending on the circumstances - when it came to running Griffin.

But nothing was going to be that easy. Boysie knew it soon after he checked in. Goldfinch went off to park the car and Lavenham saw him through the reception formalities. He had the feeling that Lavenham had orders to leech him, even accompanying him to the room, together with an uncommunicative porter who all but threw the luggage onto the bed.

Ten minutes later, after Boysie had put out his pyjamas and washed some of the dust from his hands and face, Herbie Goldfinch reappeared. Mostyn wanted to see them, and, as a trio, they trooped through to the next room along the corridor.

The first thing Boysie noticed was that the adjoining door had been unlocked. There was to be direct access between Mostyn’s room and his own.

“Well done, Oakesie. You got here. Now you stay until we have it set up for you, okay?”

He wore navy blue pants and a dark blue shirt, infuriatingly casual, sprawled in an easy chair, a drink not far from his hand, his feet shod in suede moccasins. Why was it that Boysie always regarded Mostyn’s feet with envy?

It was plain that the colonel was running the show and Boysie was not going to be let off the leash. Oh well, he sighed, as Mostyn prattled on about communications and keeping it tight, Mexico City's just another town, probably with the same bars and whores and the same dull boring people. He was sad that he would miss a peek at the old Aztec culture.

Mostyn still talked and the tiny nag of concern did not immediately bite. When it did, Boysie began to ask himself questions.

People like Lavenham and Goldfinch were in the room and Mostyn was being unusually insecure. Did those two know who he was and what he had come to do? If they did, then things were not altogether normal, for Mostyn ran Boysie with care: their meetings were always covered with cut outs and markers who were never doubled, fallbacks which were fool proof.

"You're my personal secret weapon, old love," Mostyn would say. "No other blighter will take on the responsibility so I'm landed with you. And you with me."

As though reading Boysie's anxiety, Mostyn nodded to Lavenham and Goldfinch. "See you later," he said pleasantly; though the words were patently dismissive.

Goldfinch raised his eyebrows, and the good-looking Lavenham grinned, giving a small shrug. They left the room without a word.

"Drinkies?" soothed Mostyn.

"Do they know why I'm here?"

"Not exactly. Gin, whisky, brandy, anything you like."

Boysie accepted a whisky as though he was doing his master a supreme favour.

"Do they know?" he asked again.

Mostyn smiled a smirk of superiority. "They know you're a heavy, but, as far as they're concerned, you're here to do the lifting. We've got the Frogs and the Yanks in tow. They'll think the same."

"But they'll know the truth when it's over."

Mostyn's head slowly moved from side to side. "Not if we play it right. We're going to lift them in about forty-eight hours. When we get there officially, they'll have been removed." You could not tell if it was a smile or a leer. "Removed to a better life."

Boysie looked unhappy. "And ..." he began.

"And you are the removal man, Boysie."

"They'll be suspicious."

"Not a chance. I'll be with you when we go in."

"Where are they?"

"About a hundred miles from here. Place called Puebla; we'll be going there tomorrow and you'll do your stuff either tomorrow night or in the wee smalls of the next morning."

"Where? In a hotel or where?"

"They're in an 'otel at the moment," he glanced at a note pad. "La Mansion, Puebla. Someone's keeping them in the style to which they hope to become accustomed."

"And I've got to do it there? Just like that?"

"Rooms 60 and 61. Just like that. I brought you a little present." Mostyn eased himself out of his chair and strutted across to his bedside table, opening a drawer. "Catch," the pistol arched across the room. Boysie fielded it.

"But I've got the forty-five. The Colt."

"Then I'm adjusting things a little."

Boysie looked down at the weapon. A Luger.

"Catch again."

The black tube curled over into Boysie's hand.

"It works well enough with the Luger," Mostyn closed the drawer with his hip. "There's not much you can do about noise when it comes to forty-fives, but with this it will be a case of things that go plop in the night instead of a bloody great bang."

It was all becoming very complicated. He hoped, with some apprehension, that Griffin was carrying the right equipment.

"How many of your private army are trampling over the ground?"

Mostyn, reseated in his chair, eyed Boysie's hand, carefully weighing the Luger, with distaste. "They're not trampling; they're all very experienced people."

"How many?"

"The Frog and the Yank are here," he counted off on his fingers. "The two you've already seen. There're two over in Puebla looking after our cousins, and there's a treat for you."

"What kind of a treat?" Boysie sounded wary.

Mostyn smiled a great big inviting grin: the kind of grin with which the wolf must have greeted Little Red Riding Hood's grandmother. "A bit of nookie."

"Department nookie?"

"In a way."

"Well," Boysie fingered the Luger. He would like to be in a position to use it on Mostyn. When Mostyn offered treats there was always some kind of catch. "Well, we shall see."

The telephone began to get anxious, startling Boysie so that he dropped the Luger.

"Careful with that, old love, it's Department property." Mostyn lazily reached out for the telephone. "Yes," he said into the mouthpiece. Then, "When? ... How do you know? ... Well, we've got plenty of time, haven't we? They won't be moving on until after he's arrived. You'll be pleased to know that the lifter's here and we'll take 'em out in forty-eight hours or so ... What? ... No, I do not think we should do it any sooner: besides, the travel arrangements are made. Once we take them I don't want to hang about. I can think of nothing worse than sweating in some godforsaken room, drinking tequila and eating tortillas with a couple of hot live pieces of merchandise struggling in the cupboard ... No, Martin, I'm not getting the Mexican disease ... And mañana to you, dear boy. See you tomorrow ... Oh, Martin ... *Vaya con Dios*."

This time the smile was the one selected by the wolf after he had sampled *Grandmere de le petit Chaperon rouge, chasseur*.

"It's all set up and we've got a bonus. Our fat friend, Chiliman, is arriving to pick them up on Sunday morning. Around nine o'clock. You will do them at about five so that comrade Chiliman will get there a little late."

"He'll be cross," said Boysie, his mind leaping ahead, ticking off, on mental fingers, the information he had to get to Griffin in the nearby Bamer: hotel in Puebla, room numbers, time, method.

"Very cross," mused Mostyn. "I think you had best remain incommunicado. You have a perfectly respectable room. Food will be brought to you at regular intervals. The nookie will have to wait until tomorrow night. I must now go and wallow in the Mexican fleshpots, and, judging by the girth of some of the waiters, the pots have never been fleshier."

Alone in his room he began to pace to and fro. He knew how hamsters felt in their cages, treading those abominable little wheels. He suddenly realised how tired he was: and how twitchy. The Luger lay on the bed with the sound modulator next to it. The Colt forty-five was in his case.

The bloody place was full of artillery, all he needed now was a sombrero and a couple of cartridge belts and he would be on his way to becoming a revolutionary-Mexican style.

For a minute, in the vivid fantasy area of his mind, Boysie led the peasants through the streets, having conquered the evil dictator El Supremo Mostyno. Voluptuous young women kept throwing themselves at the car, pelting him with roses, trying to climb onto the running board in order to smother their hero with warm kisses, only to be fended off by El Oakes's henchmen.

There was one particular woman, slim, dark-haired, with large brown eyes, flared nostrils and the look of a gypsy. "Thees one I'll have," El Oakes muttered, and she was dragged aboard. Then the fantasy faded and he was alone in the room knowing that he would have to do something about getting the instructions to Charlie Griffin who would, by this time, be settled into the Bamer under the name Cyril Goodlife, one of his regular aliases.

Locking the door, Boysie sat down at the dressing table, routed for paper and envelopes and began to compose a note to Griffin, which, if opened, would not entirely give the game away. It took him six goes and the final result read -

Dear Cyril,

I much enjoyed our conversation on the plane. I'm sorry but 1 will not, after all, be able to meet you and do the town as we planned. I find that business is taking me to Puebla tomorrow first thing. 1 do not know as yet where I will be staying should you be near there, but I will have to get the business finished quickly - by the early hours of Sunday morning, for instance.

You could try a hotel called La Mansion. I have some friends there, though they are not in my age group one is sixty and the other sixty-one. So I don't want to be tied up with them for long, and I should think I'll be shooting off fast and quietly.

If we don't meet again on this trip, perhaps I'll see you back in London.

Yours -

He signed his name and read it over again. Not very good, and it would not fool Mostyn for a second, but needs must.

Boysie folded the paper and put it into an envelope, sealing it and addressing it to Cyril Goodlife at the Bamer. Quietly he unlocked the door and opened it.

"You want something?" Bob Lavenham stood in the corridor.

"Ah," said Boysie without inspiration.

"The gaffer said I was to look after things," grinned Lavenham. "See you weren't disturbed and all that. Food? Drink?"

"Yes," Boysie was still uninspired. "Yes, food, I think."

Lavenham's grin broadened. "You want me to fix it, or can you manage room service? They speak English." He spoke as though addressing a not over-bright four-year-old.

Bastard, thought Boysie. That bastard Mostyn, I know what he's done: given them all the impression that I'm not fit to be out on my own. Okay, if that was the way he wanted it. "Just order me something light," he said, trying to sound superior.

"Local grub?"

"Of course."

"You sure? It can play havoc with the old bowels."

"My bowels have been likened to those of the rhinoceros."

"It's your funeral."

"Well, just have the stuff sent up."

"Okay."

Lavenham disappeared along the corridor and, for a second, Boysie thought of making a run for it, but what small amount of common sense he retained told him that was not the way. He turned back, flopped into a chair, lit a cigarette and riffled through his money. He needed a largish tip for room service if he was going to pull this one off.

Five minutes later there was a tap at the door. Lavenham stood there looking pleased with himself.

"Grub up soon."

Boysie nodded. "Good. I want to eat and rest."

"I could keep you company if you like."

"I'd rather be on my own. If I change my mind, presumably you'll be within shouting distance."

"Just outside. I feel a bit of a Charlie actually." Boysie grinned: after all it was his turn. "Good luck, Charlie."

Lavenham gave him a wry smile and retreated. Ten minutes later there was tap at the door. Boysie expected room service. Instead it was a chambermaid: dark, curving where it mattered, and with a winning smile which hurt.

"I turn down bed? Make ready for sleep?" She asked ingenuously.

Boysie's flagging loins reacted and he wanted to suggest things which would undoubtedly land him inside the nearest Mex jail. Lavenham still lurked in the corridor pretending not to notice. Boysie grinned, nodded and stepped back to let the girl in. She was dressed in black with a white apron, not unlike the French maids in cheap porno films.

She also walked with a flounce and went about her duties slowly, as though trying to draw attention to herself. Eminent jailbait, Boysie thought. Then his mind went into after burn.

If Lavenham was leeching and marking he would expect clandestine messages to be dropped cheekily in public, or via room service with a damned great tip. The chambermaid might be easier.

Boysie crossed to the writing table and retrieved the letter from under the blotter.

"You speak English?" He asked as casually as he could manage.

"Leetle," she smiled. It was the kind of smile that hit you somewhere between the heart and the genitals, just where you keep your cheque book and wallet.

"You do something for me?" It came out lecherous and she backed away.

"No-no-no," Boysie rattled. "I need a letter delivering." He flapped the envelope as though fanning himself. "You understand?"

"Yes," she looked and sounded puzzled.

"Not illegal. Nothing wrong, but big business deal," he rubbed his right thumb against the first and second fingers indicating that money was involved. That sparked interest.

"I have many business rivals. It must be private otherwise I would send it with the porter." His right hand traced to his pocket, disclosing a sizeable wad of pesos.

"Yes," the chambermaid repeated. She understood all right.

"Letter has to go to the Bamer. Now. Tonight. Nobody must see."

"I take," her smile lodged like a pocket of wind behind his ribs. She was eager. "You want me come back later?" The innocence was gone.

Boysie would have given a lot for her to come back but it was not on. He shook his head. "Just hide the letter and take it to the Bamer, soon."

The envelope passed between them, together with the pesos. She held them tightly in her hand, suddenly uncertain. Then, with an eloquent gesture, "Where I hide so nobody see?"

Boysie shrugged. That was stupid, all women have personal hidey holes: they start their secrets at school. A picture flashed into his head of the playground and a blonde girl standing close to the red brickwork with the cricket stumps chalked uncertainly nearby. The screw of paper passing between them (*Meet you top of Three Chain Hill seven o'clock*), the flash of thin thighs and dark blue underwear and the note gone, deposited with the handkerchief and chewing gum and god knew what else.

The chambermaid did her female ESP act, drooped her head, looked up at him under the eyelashes and fluttered. Then her hands swooped down to the hem of the black dress.

Boysie felt the personal bitter lakes of sweat break out as the envelope and money vanished: the long legs as sweet as any illicit peek, bringing on the hot flush. He was short of breath.

"I come back," the girl repeated.

"No," Boysie said firmly.

She gave a little sigh and pulled a face. "Okay, I deliver letter. No trouble."

She left, Boysie in a state wishing that female company could be allowed.

A little later, room service arrived - a large and blue jowled waiter wheeling a trolley loaded with food, one bottle and a brace of tumblers.

"Okay," said the waiter giving him a big twinkle which turned sour as Boysie signed the bill and discovered that all his loose change had gone to the chambermaid.

"I'll see you later," Boysie made it sound sincere. "*Si*," he was unconvinced, and left throwing looks like poisoned darts.

Boysie turned his attention to the food. He suspected that it was Mexican food for tourists. There was a kind of salad and some chicken in a spicy sauce. He picked at the food and drank a considerable amount of the booze -an unidentifiable wine, with a jazzy label.

Boysie had consumed his third glass when two events occurred simultaneously. There was a rap at the door and the telephone began to ring. Boysie froze, unable to work out the logistics of the situation. After a few seconds, which seemed to take a couple of hours, he plumped for the door. Lavenham leaned against the jamb.

"Have pity for a poor struggler out in the cold." Why in hell did Lavenham never stop grinning? "Your telephone's ringing," he added unnecessarily.

"Oh, come in if you have to," Boysie leaped from the door to the phone.

"Hallo."

"Mr. Oakes?" Griffin, furtive at the far end of the line.

"Yes ... No, I think you have the wrong room."

"You mean you can't talk?" persisted Griffin.

"Mmmm."

"What's the form? Answer yes or no."

It took Boysie a second to work out that the question was not one easily answered by the negative or affirmative.

"Are our friends in town?" Griffin sounded more stealthy than ever.

"No," firmly. Then, lower key, "You've got a wrong number."

"Where are they then? What's the score?"

Boysie's mental agility leaped to Olympic heights. "Note?" he said loudly, "What note? I know nothing about writing a note to you. Who are you anyway?"

"You mean you've sent a note to me?"

"Yes. I'm very sorry, you've got a wrong number, I really can't help you anymore."

"Mr. Oakes, look, I ..."

Boysie had cradled the receiver. "Some freak," he muttered to Lavenham who had stopped smiling.

"It's bloody embarrassing, lurking in that corridor," Lavenham took a couple of steps forward.

"You shouldn't have joined them, should you?"

"Oh, come on, we're all in the same boat."

"Not me, chum," Boysie had his bolshie mood firmly in position. "I do this for Uncle Mostyn all the time. It's like this on every operation:

sitting around in bloody hotels, jetting all over the place - instant boredom alleviated only by short bursts of terror."

"You're a pretty heavy bloke then?" It could have been rhetorical. "Mind if I have a drink?" That one was rhetorical: Lavenham had already picked up the bottle.

"Help yourself." It was time to cover himself, Boysie thought. Time for some studied fiction. "I don't know about being heavy. It's like working as a bailiff. I'm a kind of mobile arresting officer. I'm told I've got the build for it."

"You often get wrong numbers on your phone?" Lavenham was jumpy about that telephone call.

"I wouldn't know, I haven't been here long enough to find out. What's Mostyn's game, anyway, keeping me trussed up?"

"You're not trussed."

"Well, cooped then."

"I gather it's an edgy situation. He doesn't want you to go missing before the main event."

Boysie looked aimless and artless. "I never did before."

"Jesus, what vile booze," Lavenham took a long pull at his drink. "I don't think he's really worried about you, but he has some heavy competition leaning in his direction."

"The Yanks and the Frogs."

"Reputations at stake. Heads likely to roll. You know how it is."

"Not really, I'm only a cash-and-carry man myself." Boysie settled back into his chair. "How did you get into the filth trade?" He knew it was a *verboten* question, but the best form of defence was attack. Keep them thinking about themselves and they might lose you.

"You sound like a classic whore's client," Lavenham raised his eyebrows.

"Aren't we all classic clients? Or classic whores? It's a similar trade: we use ponces, dirty postcards, street corners, window displays, whips, the kinky stuff, two-way mirrors, bedbugs, flashers. You ever work with Mostyn when he's pulling a bit of black?"

"Yes," Lavenham appeared lost in thought. "Yes, I have. I suppose you're right."

Silence, apart from some music a long way off and filtered noises from the street.

"How did you get in?" Boysie repeated the question.

Lavenham returned to consciousness. "Me? I was at the end of an army contract, trying to make up my mind whether to sign on for another term. They asked me if I fancied DPI and I thought I might give it a whirl, so they began vetting." He paused.

"Where?" inserted Boysie.

"Berlin. It was uncanny. People used to turn up uninvited and talk about things I had forgotten long ago. I felt as though they'd pinned some kind of notice on my back, like at school, you know ..."

"Kick me." Boysie chuckled, nodding.

"That's it. Then, one morning Mostyn arrived. Don't ask me how he knew, simply waltzed into my office and said he'd heard about the DPI vetting and thought he might be able to offer me a better deal."

"That's his style. Mostyn likes poaching: very handy with the gaff."

Lavenham sighed. "Yes. It got a mite hairy."

"DPI gamekeepers?"

"They ran me all over the place. You know the routine."

"Know it? I've been part of it."

"In desperation I said yes to Mostyn and everything changed. Red carpet. A special aircraft laid on."

"England, home and beauty."

"England. Not home, though. Rather the GPO."

The GPO Executive Training Centre, a Hampshire manor house with extensive grounds, was cover for the Department Prep School. Everyone disappeared there from time to time: it was where you learned the theory and how to handle the hardwear. Later they took you to Whitehall to learn the politics on the ground. In Hampshire they bled you of any preconceived political ideals.

"We all share that experience."

"It's a job. Somebody has to do it."

Boysie leered like a shark. "Then don't beef if you have to wait outside my room all night."

Lavenham was a nice enough bloke, Boysie thought. Under different circumstances they would have got along well enough, but not on this one when he was playing both ends against the middle: and certainly not at this time of night. He was tired and needed rest. God knew if Griffin would get his message, via the chambermaid's honeydew thighs, or if he would be able to read between the lines, or even get to the right hotel in the right town at the right time, let alone the right rooms. If he did not, then Boysie would be left holding the baby. Tomorrow might prove exceeding dodgy.

"You want me out?" asked Lavenham.

"When you've finished your drink. No hurry, but I want to get some Egyptian PT."

Lavenham chuckled. "Bash the old charpoy, what?"

"Right," said Boysie, brightly, and with a certain amount of determination.

Before getting into bed, Boysie checked out the Luger, made sure the thing was loaded, screwed the silencer in place and slipped the piece into his bedside drawer. He then had one last go at setting his mind at rest regarding Griffin. The hotel switchboard had him linked into the Bamer switchboard in no time, but they could raise no response from Griffin's room. They were courteous enough, and even asked if he would like them to page Mr. Goodlife, but Boysie decided that was pushing things a little far. For all he knew, Mostyn could be dining at the Bamer.

When exhaustion at last banished consciousness, Boysie dreamed vividly and in technicolour. Six very fat Mexican waiters were approaching him, each holding a leg of chicken in a menacing fashion. The legs of chicken were equipped with silencers and the whole affair was being watched by Mostyn and Griffin. When they got near to him, the waiters pressed the triggers on their legs of chicken and squirted Boysie with sauce.

He woke in a sweat and with stomach ache which, in turn, led to uncontrollable diarrhoea.

VII - DISCORD

Opposite to concord jarring chord, thus requiring a resolution to another chord

Herbie Goldfinch was at the wheel with Boysie sitting next to him while Mostyn lounged in the back, flanked by the Frenchman, Grenot, and the American, Smith. Outside the comfort of the air-conditioned convertible, it was searingly hot and clear. Nobody spoke much, and Lavenham, who had seen them off from the hotel, appeared to be relieved at their departure.

Boysie had been introduced to Grenot and Smith only ten minutes before they were due to leave, and neither the Frenchman, nor the tall ugly American seemed impressed: rather they regarded Boysie with some distaste.

As for Boysie, he was too depressed to be concerned by Grenot and Smith's lack of enthusiasm, for he ached with that kind of gloom which always follows in the wake of an acute disorder of the bowels. The raw vacuum had yet to adjust and he was uncertain about the possibilities of ever actually consuming food again.

Throughout the seventy-five mile journey there was little conversation, only matters of importance and a brief exchange between Mostyn and the two in the back, with Mostyn explaining tactics.

"Just as long as we get them out," commented Smith after listening to Mostyn's careful situation analysis.

"I do not care 'ow it is done," the Frenchman said firmly. "What matters is that it has to be done and seen to be done."

"No sweat," Mostyn appeared to be at ease. "We're very experienced in these matters and it's only got to be seen once we've got 'em safely back to Paris."

Boysie glanced into the mirror on the passenger side and saw an infuriating smile playing around Mostyn's pinguid lips. Sod him, thought Boysie, sod the sodding perisher. Oakes, my lad, you're being set up. If anyone carries the can for this nest of bees it is not going to be Mostyn, wily bastard that he is: the shit will undoubtedly land on Brian Ian-Boysie-Oakes.

It took a little under two hours to complete their journey, with only four stops at gasoline stations - not for gasoline, but at Boysie's urgent request in order to avail himself of the conveniences provided. As an operative for the Department of Special Security, Boysie reflected, he would make a damned good compost heap.

By mid-afternoon they pulled in among the oblong houses of the old colonial city of Puebla, and, within half-an-hour, Boysie was settled into his room at the Palace - nicely appointed, clean and neat with, he noted straight away, a double bed.

It did not come as a surprise to discover that he was the only member of the party billeted at the Palace, which was only a block away from La Mansion where Pinkney and Defoe were snug in rooms sixty and sixty-one.

There was nothing to do but sit and wait. After all, Boysie considered, nobody was going anywhere without him. He stretched out on the bed, the Luger within reach, and drifted into an uneasy doze.

He woke with a start, wondering how long the tapping at the door had been going on. The sun was flushing blood red through the window blind and his watch showed five-thirty. Holding the Luger behind his right thigh, Boysie made the door in four easy strides. Mostyn was on the other side, looking petulant.

"What the hell's wrong with you, Oakes? I've been knocking for five minutes."

Boysie held the door open to let his small superior pass into the room.

"I'm bloody worn out," he said wearily. "You know what's wrong with me, I've been up half the night - a touch of Montezuma's revenge."

Mostyn eyed him up and down, after the manner of the headwaiter of the Savoy Grill greeting a drunken tramp.

"You'll have to put Montezuma in his place, you're on at five tomorrow morning." He slumped into a chair. "Think you'll wake up in time for that episode?"

"Nothing a couple of brandies won't cure." He nodded towards a small drinks cabinet, complete with refrigerator, in the corner by the balcony window.

“Lay off the booze,” Mostyn clipped sharply. “I don’t want you raving drunk running around this town. The law here can be very mean.”

“Five o’clock in the morning,” sighed Boysie. “Will you have your goons out of sight by then?”

“They’ll be tucked away in their beddie-byes. I call them off at four-thirty. Martin and Nick Holborn,” Mostyn added vaguely.

“As long as they keep out of my way.”

“We go in, theoretically, at eight,” Mostyn paused for a bleak smile. “At about eight-five we return to break the bad news to our continental and transatlantic cousins.”

Mostyn went on, showing Boysie the street plan and how to get to La Mansion. It appeared that some small bribery had taken place and there would be nobody in the lobby around five o’clock; there would, however, be a pass key lying on the reception counter.

“Don’t cock it up, lad, will you?” was Mostyn’s parting shot.

Boysie swallowed hard. If Griffin was there it would not be cocked up. If he did not make it, then Boysie would have to screw up his own courage, a feat of some acrobatic proportions when it concerned taking action in cold blood.

He sighed, feeling the anxiety creatures mingling with the indiscreet microbes which were going through their death throes in his guts. Sitting on the bed once more, Boysie pondered over the advisability of taking any nourishment before embarking into the unknown, his active imagination clicking through the permutations: if he ate and the bowels were operating on a chain reaction system, there could be serious repercussions. If Griffin, for instance, did not turn up, there would be hell to pay: whoever heard of an assassin unable to complete a hit because, at the crucial moment, his sphincter let him down? It just did not happen. Yet, Boysie was well aware that his stomach was empty and some of the pain was now due to hunger.

He stretched out again, feeling sleepy once more, a not unnatural reaction in the circumstances: it was as though his body was placing his mind in a *Too Difficult* tray.

The room was in almost complete darkness when he woke the second time, and the tapping was now of a different nature: not the urgent raps of Mostyn, but a more gentle, hesitant knock.

Boysie repeated his previous actions, on this occasion blundering into a chair in the semi-darkness and barking his shin.

A girl stood at the door. Tall, slender, her face too angular to be called beautiful, but with blue clear eyes and fair hair worn almost to her shoulders. There was a hint of Arpege in the air, drifting between them, and he did not imagine the mocking glint in her eyes.

"Can I come in?" the voice pleasant and low.

"Depends. Don't I know you from somewhere?"

"We've met before. Don't you ever spare an eye for the hired help?"

It figured. She was one of the many receptionists at the Whitehall office. He recognised her now, and the symptoms which built inside him. Strictly speaking, operatives were forced to give the secretarial staff a wide berth, a situation which always made those cool languorous ladies more desirable. You always want what you cannot have, as Boysie knew to his cost.

He stepped back, holding the door open for her. She came in, with the steady, almost haughty, stride you could see any day in the upper echelon Department offices, or accompanying captains of power to their Rolls-Royces in the City. Boysie sneered inside. He knew the type: out of reach, but only just - very frustrating.

She wore striking light blue cool silk ending just above the knee, tight at the waist and no slack across the bust.

"What're you doing out in the field? Number Two got some correspondence to dictate or something?"

A tic in the rear of his head because this could be the promised nookie, and if it was, then Mostyn was definitely up to no good.

"I'm being given a chance to work out of the office."

She went straight across to the same easy chair in which Mostyn had sat, arranging herself with some grace, crossing her legs and letting the hemline ride up.

"Welcome to the club. What can I do for you?"

"You can give me a drink, first. Our mutual friend and master has banned me from his company and suggested that you might like someone to talk with. Are you under house arrest or something?"

The question was so blatantly innocuous that Boysie felt irritated.

"You know bloody well I'm not," he snapped.

"Drink, then. Gin," she said with a whisper of a smile.

"Tonic?"

"Please."

Boysie fixed the drinks, pouring himself a liberal brandy from some bottle he did not recognise.

"It's unforgivable, I know, but I've forgotten your name."

"I don't suppose you ever knew it: terribly pedestrian - Joan, would you believe Joan Palmer?"

"The Berkshire Palmers?" Boysie raised a quizzical eyebrow.

This time there was not even a twinkle. "Wiltshire actually," flat.

Joan Palmer obviously took her lineage seriously: another bad sign, because Mostyn was also stuffy about things like that. Right background, right breeding, right clubs. All most important to people like Mostyn and, presumably, the Palmer girl.

Boysie sipped at the brandy. It burned horribly, hitting the wounded stomach like phosphorous, making him gasp slightly.

"Are you all right?"

Boysie nodded, tight-lipped. "The Aztecs are waging a minor skirmish with my stomach. Mopping up operations, that's all."

"That should kill anything," she inclined her head towards the brandy.

"I think they probably use it as a cleansing fluid." Boysie took another sip. It did not hurt so much this time. "So, you're learning how to operate in the field."

"I'm learning how to wait in hotel rooms and not ask awkward questions."

"That's what I said. You want to eat?"

"I've eaten. You?"

"Not wise."

"What do you suggest then, Snap? Happy Families?"

"Happy Families is always good for a laugh, only I haven't brought my cards. Anyway I'm short on Mr. Snoop and Spy and Mrs. Hump the ..."

"Enough," she raised a hand, mock shock on her face.

They fenced on for about an hour, talking in circles, avoiding life at the Department and the current operation, about which, Boysie suspected, she knew far too much. It was mainly Mummy, Daddy and schooldays stuff - how she had coped with this crush developed in the sixth form for some actor ("All my friends had pictures of film stars on their lockers, I felt very superior because he was a *classical* actor. I think the nuns approved.")

Another couple of brandies and Boysie's stomach was anaesthetised. The alcohol was putting him on: being alone, at night, in an hotel room with a woman, helped.

At last he said, "Mind if I lie down for a while?"

"You want me to leave you alone?"

"Threat or promise?"

"I'd like to stay. It's been a lonely trip."

"Then stay," the pause was minimal. "Lie down and rest as well if you like." Cheeky.

He did not seriously expect the reaction, even though Mostyn had made the vague promise. She smiled, stood up, crossed to the door and locked it. Then she began to undress.

The underwear was pretty and expensive, but not erotic - none of your Soho fake whore stuff on sale for the randy housewife. Nor was she as angular, stripped, as she appeared fully dressed, the flesh being allocated in neat and rounded proportions: the stomach flat, taut as a bongo head; breasts without a hint of sag, and no hard protrusion of hip bones at the terminal concave of her waist; the thighs were slender with no heaviness, their junction marked by a minimum soft light down which did not fuzz or bush.

She came to him slowly, her hand reaching for the switch on the big bedside lamp.

"Prudish?" Boysie asked with a grin.

"I concentrate better in the dark," she breathed.

"Very old fashioned."

"Mmmm, I know," she nestled close, starting to unbutton his shirt, her fingers like a set of vibrators. "In my experience it's a good variation; all my friends want to prove things in the light."

She paid a lot of attention to his nipples, like a man might work on a woman. Boysie wondered, fragmentarily, if she was AC/DC. If that was her particular thing, she was certainly extremely well balanced. Three times, in spite of Boysie's recent indisposition and he could not deny that the potency was mainly her doing: San Francisco 1906; Mont Pelée 1929; and a mild tremor somewhere or other, probably in the Ionian Islands.

***

The thunderhead was about four miles to the west of Puebla. It broke, with all its attendant drama, at around four in the morning. Boysie did not hear it, and the thunder was only a distant rumble when Joan Palmer gently woke him at four-thirty.

"It's time you were getting ready, Boysie. Time to go." His vision was bleared, the light bright in his eyes; somewhere nearby there was the tinkle of china.

"Coffee, Boysie. You've got time for coffee. It's four-thirty."

Gold-flecked wallpaper. He raised himself on one elbow, catching sight of the pair of paintings above the big bedside lamp: reproductions, bold pieces by some modern Mexican artist.

She was holding out the cup of coffee, hair hanging over one side of her face, tousled. She had put her panties back on. Modesty? Boysie wondered. Then his stomach turned over as he realised what he had to do in the next half hour or so.

"It's pouring with rain," she told him. That accounted for the hiss and drip of which he was vaguely aware. He rubbed his eyes again and took the coffee, looking round the room. His clothes had been neatly folded on one of the chairs. He squinted at his watch, realising that he would have to move fast. If Griffin ... but then he did not dare to think about Griffin.

They did not speak much as Boysie dressed, slipped into the lightweight raincoat and checked the Luger in the bathroom.

Joan Palmer lay on the bed, sipping coffee and looking solemn.

"You'll wait 'till I get back?"

"Of course," she inclined her head. Impeccable, thought Boysie: great breeding and great breeding stock. She would make a super wife for one of the chinless wonders one of these days, but some lucky lover would pilfer the erotic profits.

"See you then," he scooped up his key and left.

The walk from the Palace to La Mansion took only seven minutes, but Boysie was sodden by the time he reached the pavement across the road from the hotel's facade, the rain coming down straight, in big drops as though some archangel had opened a stop-cock on the celestial shower bath.

There were lights on and no sign of life - except for the car out front: a grey Citroen, the DS 19, with someone at the wheel.

Boysie sank back into what shadow there was, sank being the operative word for the water, bouncing up from the pavement, had slurped into his shoes. It was like walking in a paddling pool.

The Citroen should not have been there; nor the man at the wheel, a bulky man, Boysie judged in the poor light, fat, squat and, probably, short.

The second hand on his watch was sweeping the seconds and minutes away. Time was irreversible for Pinkney, Defoe, and, though he did not like the thought, Boysie.

The fat man in the Citroen started the motor, his head turned towards the plate glass and steel-framed doors to the hotel's lobby.

More movement: someone coming out, walking in a determined manner, then breaking into a trot, presumably to avoid the drops, between which you could not have got a matchstick. The man coming out was wearing a white suit and there was a flash of red coming from the shirt neck. The guy did not have much taste in ties. Dark hair, slick; swarthy face, Boysie doubted if he could ever pick him out again.

The car pulled away, the expensive engine note dropping as he turned the corner, the plashing whisper of rubber on the wet road diminished until all was quiet again. Boysie's watch showed two minutes past five.

Without rushing it, he crossed the road, wiping his face with a handkerchief as he came into the protection of the concrete awning above the glass entrance doors.

The lobby was deserted, though there was a small light flashing red on the switchboard visible behind the reception desk. At the far end, the lights above two elevators showed that both cars were down.

Boysie screwed up his discipline, willing his legs to go slow, stopping himself from breaking into a panicky run to the reception desk. He was half-a-dozen paces from it by the time he saw the key, lying forlorn on one of the three blotters. He reached forward, scooped it up, moving to the right and heading towards the elevator.

Inside the car, with the button pressed to *six*, Boysie realised that his breathing was laboured, hands unsteady and his own heartbeat over-riding everything else. The tic in the left corner of his mouth was fully active and he now knew that he could not rely on Montezuma having been overcome by the local brandy.

The sixth floor corridor was deserted - a bad sign. Cursing, he realised that he should have taken a few seconds longer in reception, to peek at the guest list and see if Griffin was registered. But there was not time for that now. He was committed; if Griffin had not done it, then Boysie would have to force himself. He felt dangerously sick.

There was a pair of shoes, brown and ranged hopefully outside room sixty; there was no sound from inside. Boysie clutched the key in his left hand and let his right curl around the Luger, still entrenched in the pocket of his raincoat - a misnomer, obvious from its sagging impregnated condition.

He slid the key quietly into the lock, turning clockwise until he felt pressure. As he drew the Luger out of his pocket, surplus rainwater ran in rivulets down the barrel.

He slid the safety off, holding the weapon close to his body, the muzzle angled towards the door.

Fear, like a clutch of tarantulas, crawled up the back of his neck and the nausea rose in his gorge. Then, a deep breath, all muscles tense: thumb and forefinger twisted on the key and he pushed forward, the Luger raised and ready as he moved, his left hand reaching out to where he supposed the light switch would be.

There was no need for the switch: the lights were full on. Neither was there any need for the weapon. The occupant of room sixty was already dead, smashed across the bed with his head back and a wound the size of a tangerine in his throat. There was a lot of blood and the room smelled foul.

Boysie threw up.

It took only a few seconds for him to wipe his mouth and back out of the room, removing the key and leaning against the wall outside, but it seemed like an hour.

"You got here then." Griffin was standing about five feet away, between the rooms.

Boysie's gun hand came up, then relaxed. He breathed out, expelling the air from his lungs, ridding himself of tension. "You did it then?"

"What?"

"Rooms sixty and sixty-one."

"Just going to, I've had hell's own job getting a pass key. Almost had to go a full five rounds with a bloody nympho chambermaid. But it's okay now," Griffin brandished the fruits of victory.

About twenty seconds passed before the truth dawned. "Someone's done it," said Boysie.

"Not you?" Griffin asked, suspicion edging into his voice, creased round his eyes.

"Not on your ... No. But someone's done that one. I don't know about the other."

Griffin eyed the Luger with even greater mistrust. "Better have a look."

He turned to the door of sixty-one, slipping the key into the lock, working with surprising speed and silence. Boysie saw the glint of something in the undertaker's right hand, then Griffin was inside the room.

"Bloody scab labour," he said emerging with a hurt expression, closing the door behind him. "It's all tied up. I've come all this way for nothing."

"Best get out then," Boysie had jammed the Luger back into his pocket. "See you back in London."

"You'd better. I expect the rest of my cut."

They left, fast and separately, Boysie going first. There was nobody watching: not that he spotted anyway. Nor did he meet anyone on the way back to the Palace; and there was nobody in his room when he finally closed the door behind him, feeling the jelly in his legs and the hornets idling their motors in his guts. The sweats were back and he leaned heavily against the door. But there was no Joan Palmer to ease him into the bath and lift the depression by letting him try to make it back to the oblivion of the womb.

He cleaned himself up and tried for sleep, but it came only in small gobbets, the darkness punctuated by sudden startled alertness in which he was aware of his heart thumping against his ribs.

Mostyn came in at eight. "I gather it all went off very well," he said as if talking of some cocktail party, or Queen Charlotte's Ball.

Boysie preferred not to answer. Mostyn could believe what he liked.

"Time for the histrionics, then," Mostyn chivvied as Boysie climbed into his clothes, ran a razor over his chin and splashed his face with aftershave.

They walked over to La Mansion, retracing the route Boysie had taken during the night. The place was alive, cordonned by fat and corrupt-looking coppers with their weaponry slung low. Others were arriving in large American cars, and there was a crowd of rubberneckers.

They made it look good, for the sake of any French or American markers who might have been gathered for the big match. Mostyn made a bit of a bru-ha-ha and Boysie ran interference. There was some pushing and general unpleasantness.

Back at the Palace, where they were joined by Grenot and Smith, the real row began. The Frenchman and American became white-faced and tight-lipped at first. Boysie thought that it was going to be all right, but the scene began to build once they were all in the car, on the way back to Mexico City.

To start with they blamed Mostyn, but he turned all their assaults neatly, and in the end they blamed each other. Mostyn, persistent to the finish, let it be known that in his opinion the whole thing was down to Smith and the Americans.

"It bears the stamp of your lot," he snarled angrily. "Things get difficult and you panic. You brought your triggers in didn't you?"

"What about the goon you're carrying?" Smith spat back.

"I'm a bring 'em back alive boy," Boysie said coolly, proud of himself.

"Don't worry. I know about you," Smith countered.

The last half-hour of the journey was conducted in granite silence strong with unspoken threats. Forty-eight hours later they were back in London where Boysie collected his usual bonus, dropped Griffin's money off in their safe letterbox and swanned away on a private idyll with the dusky Vita whom he rescued from the jungle of Notting Hill Gate.

In eleven years the operation had never been backtracked. He saw Joan Palmer a couple of times, dined her once at Chez Solange and did not seek the comfort of her body. He bumped into Herbie Goldfinch on several occasions in the corridors of power, and was involved in one operation that also included Lavenham.

But nobody mentioned Mexico. Not until now.

VIII - LYRIC

Words of a song: originally vocal with lyre

The silence in Mostyn's room was almost tangible. It took Boysie a second or two to pull himself out of the time warp into which his mind had been deflected. He looked at each of the faces in turn: Mostyn, Charlie Griffin, Lyric Lavenham, and Couperose. This was Paris, not Puebla; 1975 not 1964. Eleven years after.

"Eleven years," he said aloud and softly.

"Over a decade," Mostyn echoed. "A decade and seven lives."

"How did they get clobbered?"

Mostyn lit a cigarette, taking his time. Griffin was up and going towards the drinks trolley again; Lyric did not move, and Gerard Couperose appeared to shift his weight from one buttock to the other.

Boysie took a deep pull at his drink.

"It started about a year ago," Mostyn began. "Joan Palmer was working for the section in New York. She shared an apartment with another girl-from the embassy. The roommate came home late, from a date, one night, and found the door lock smashed. Joan was in the bedroom. Drowned."

"In the bedroom?"

"It had been done in the bath. They had dried her off, dressed her and laid her out. That was why it didn't seem political at the time : a standard maniac freak killing."

"Jesus," breathed Boysie. The image of Joan Palmer's face floating above him in the hotel room at Puebla, her body, enthusiasm, and the darkness on which she had insisted.

"We didn't know for certain until Bob." Mostyn at least had the grace to shoot a respectful look towards Lyric. "But he was the fourth. Nick Holborn and Herbie Goldfinch were the next. They were working together, a routine matter for DI6 last May, in London. They went back to Herbie's place off the Fulham Road, for a drink about eleven one night when they'd finished. They didn't check in for a couple of days and their head of section sent a legman round to see what'd happened. Nobody'd heard a bloody thing, but there they were, sitting in easy chairs looking surprised. They each had a bullet straight through the throat, fired at close range."

"Then Bob Lavenham?" asked Boysie. He knew about bullets through the throat; he had seen one in La Mansion, Puebla.

Mostyn gave Lyric a quick look again. She nodded, acquiescently.

"Last September, in his Knightsbridge flat. Unpleasant. I won't go into details, but the joker was beginning to leave clues. There was a tape on his stereo machine. Copeland's *El Salon Mexico*: Utah Symphony Orchestra."

"Smith came from Utah. I remember that."

"I wish somebody else had. He got aerated with a scatter gun on the steps of a rooming house on the West Side of New York a month later."

"And Martin?"

"Poor old Martin. He took his car straight off the M1 and into a flyover support."

"Not an accident?"

"Someone had syphoned off his brake fluid."

"Always a good way unless someone bothers to look," Griffin muttered professionally.

"Then last December, here, in Paris, someone got at Grenot: with a knife. They found him leaking all over his living room. And that, Boysie, leaves two little Indians, you and me - if you don't count Charlie Griffin."

"And I'd rather not be counted, Colonel Mostyn, thank you." Griffin looked serious.

Boysie leaned back and closed his eyes. When he spoke it was as though his voice had somehow become detached from his body. "No clues? No leads?"

"The various police departments, and forces, concerned have swapped notes. There appear to be some similarities. Yes, Boysie, it could well have been one man, with suitable back-up operators and a control. That's really the first thing we have on the agenda."

"Sleuthing?"

"A small matter of interrogation."

"Yes?" Boysie looked up. Mostyn was on his feet, and Couperose had lifted himself from his chair. He was approaching Boysie with some menace.

"Now look here," Boysie was slow, but not that slow. "If you think I had anything to do with ..."

"Just shut up and answer a few questions." Couperose looked really unpleasant.

"I haven't been out of England since that last bloody stupid airline thing." Boysie bridled, rising and taking up a belligerent stance. He was a big man and knew the tricks. He was always ready to push it if roused. For some reason Couperose roused him.

"Steady on," Mostyn surprisingly cool. "Nobody's making accusations. But the killings have all got style, élan. You're in the business, you know the form. We simply want to know if anyone's approached you."

"Nobody approaches me, except you. Other people get approached though. Christ, Mostyn, think about it. In my early days you even fingered Griffin for me. You were high and bloody mighty then: you said the Department needed an unknown. Griffin was known. You want to ask Griffin who approaches him."

"Don't think we haven't."

"I'm in the clear." Griffin looked decidedly pleased with himself.

"Well, nobody's been in touch with me. You have my word. I reckon it's Chiliman you ought to sniff out. He stood to lose most."

"More than you know." Mostyn was subsiding again, though Couperose still hovered. "It's the obvious conclusion: the revenge motif. Don't worry, Oakes, we're looking for Chiliman, and while you're at it, I'd advise you to show a mite of respect. I could have left you out there in the cold. Just let Chiliman and his goons catch up with you. You could have ended up on the slab, Boysie, my lad, with the same surprised look as the others, wondering who had done you and why."

"Maybe I would have preferred it that way."

Mostyn took no notice. "Instead of which, I take the trouble to bring you in, warn you, put you with friends. At least in a small pack we stand a little chance."

Boysie grunted. "Do we have to attend this conference?"

"Not really. Only as a token."

"Then why Paris?"

"Because this was the spiritual home of Clambake and because we think Chiliman might just be here. He would hardly let an opportunity like this slip through his pudgy little fingers, would he?"

"That's all really cheerful. You have to bloody con me, Mostyn, in your usual slimy creeping way. You couldn't just come to me and tell me someone was going to hit me. Now that would have made sense. I could have got the hell out."

"There's no place to run to anymore."

"I'd have found somewhere. How about Scunthorpe? Nobody in their right mind would have searched for me in Scunthorpe."

"We're not talking about anyone in their right mind." That put a stop on the conversation. Boysie saw the eternal wisdom of the remark. If Chiliman, or whoever it was, had a mind to obliterate everyone concerned with the Puebla business, nothing would stop him now.

"What was Clambake anyway?"

"A lot of operation."

"But what?"

Mostyn looked nervous. Boysie suddenly felt happy. He did not remember when he had seen Mostyn looking so twitchy.

"It must have meant one hell of a lot to old Chiliman if he's flipped over it."

"His entire career, I should imagine."

"Yes," Griffin looked sad. "He started a new career, didn't he? Liquidating you lot."

"An enormous grudge, Colonel," Couperose shifted again - left buttock to right. "Do you know why? Can't you give us any detail? Or haven't we been cleared?" He sneered, "Or, perhaps it is Oakes who gets cleared."

Mostyn twitched again. "Maybe he does. But I'd have to get authorisation. Maybe I'll call London." He wrinkled his brow as though in deep and difficult thought. "Yes, Boysie, you should know about Clambake. You should know why Chiliman - if it is Chiliman - wants to get rid of us."

Boysie was suspicious. Mostyn just did not behave like this : it was not his style.

"Well, I'm off to see an old mate," Griffin rose. "That is if it's all right by everyone else."

"Keep your eyes open." Mostyn closed and opened his own lids like a lazy reptile.

"And I must check in," Couperose shrugged. "You know the arrangements. We have experienced agents looking out for all of you. They are very *discret. I* will return in an hour or so. You will be all right?"

"I've been all right for more years than I wish to remember," Mostyn sounded a shade sharp. "I can do without a nanny for a few hours. In any case, I've got some calls to make."

Couperose nodded.

"And I'm going to have a bath," announced Lyric.

Boysie felt uneasy. This was not the first time Mostyn had set him up. Instinct told him this could be another set-up and he did not like it. Certainly he did not feel like sitting in the room they had given to him: too many overhanging buildings. Whoever had done the others was very good and an overhung hotel bedroom would present little difficulty.

"Think I'll do the same," he said aloud and cheerfully. "I feel a bit sticky."

He hung his hands, rubbing the palms with his fingers to indicate the need for bathing. Surprised, he realised that he did need a bath: he could feel the sweat building in his armpits, beginning to trickle down his side.

"I'd like you back in an hour." Mostyn did not look at him as he said it.

"To tell me about Clambake?"

"Possibly. One hour, Oakesie. Right?"

"Right," said Boysie, turning towards the door.

He was the last to leave. Outside, the corridor was empty except for Lyric who stood in front of her door, at the far end, nearest the lift, juggling the key.

Boysie; never one to pass up an opportunity, grinned and set off towards her, trying to look casual but loping at speed none the less.

"You really going to have a bath?" he asked as he came close.

"Unless you've got other ideas."

He could not tell whether it was an invitation or a pinch of sarcasm. It was a sign of his encroaching middle age: he just could not distinguish anymore. Twice in the past year he had been put in embarrassing situations by wrongly interpreting young women's reactions.

"Food?" he tried tentatively.

"What a super idea. Can you give me a couple of minutes?"

Boysie looked at his watch. "Which two would you like?"

"Idiot. Come in and wait for me."

Lyric's room was better than either his or. Mostyn's. More feminine, somehow. The French knew about these matters, Boysie thought.

"I can't offer you anything." Another hint in her eyes?

"Don't worry, we can get a drink before we eat."

"I won't keep you a minute." She made for the bathroom with Boysie's eyes leeched to the long thoroughbred legs.

Come to think of it, he mused, in the last year he had about as much of a sex life as a flasher in Iceland. Miss Lyric Lavenham stirred old desires and it was a comfort to know that they were still there.

She emerged from the bathroom a couple of minutes later. In that space of time Boysie had gone through a whole fantasy seduction sequence which left him feeling slightly ashamed. He also realised that he was about to leave the hotel without any protection, apart from the French agents mentioned by Couperose.

"My turn to be difficult," he said brightly. "Must dash back to my room for a second. Can you hang on?"

She nodded, going to the wardrobe and taking out a suede coat, military in cut and the colour of crushed raspberries.

Boysie hurried down the corridor, unlocked his room and moved rapidly, unlocking his case, checking out the Baby Browning, slapping the magazine in place, snapping back the slide in the standard loading operation and slipping the catch to safety. He transferred the weapon to his hip pocket, patted his hair and returned to Lyric's room.

She was standing by the door, waiting.

"You know this part of town?"

"Not really," Boysie took her elbow, "but there's bound to be a reasonable restaurant to hand. I don't fancy staying in the hotel, unless of course ..."

"No, it looks like we'll be trapped in here for long enough on this trip anyway."

"Okay."

They found a small restaurant down the Avenue Kleber, towards the Place Charles De Gaulle, and ate pâté, escalopes de veau à la jardiniere and flan aux abricots à l'alsacienne. During the meal they shared a bottle of Château-du-Breuil and talked easily.

"I'm sorry about Bob," Boysie said towards the beginning of the veal. "I didn't know him well, but ..."

"But he was like most people in this business. A cold, hard bastard." She said it with a fond smile and without venom.

"Yes," the wind dropping from his sails. "And how long have you been in the business?"

Lyric laughed. "Not long. But long enough."

"Am I allowed to ask what you do?"

"Mainly courier work. I haven't graduated to the wheedling-secrets-out-of-visiting-diplomats brigade yet."

"Nor do you want to." Boysie had met some of those superannuated whores.

She pouted. "It's a tough game, if they tell me to do that, then I suppose I'll do it. Do you feel good about your side?"

"I haven't worked my side for a long while. I've been out, retired, grazing for years now."

"Does that help you to sleep easy?"

"I rarely sleep easy. What would you know anyway?"

"I'm told you used to slay people - on purpose."

Boysie shrugged. "Don't believe all you hear."

"You don't look like a standard heavy."

Boysie chewed on his meat and grinned. "You don't look like a standard courier. Tell me something, who recruited you?"

"Colonel Mostyn."

"When?"

"A couple of years ago."

Boysie chewed some more. "Funny that, he's supposed to have been out for about the same time as me-except for one minor excursion back. Watch yourself, Lyric, Mostyn's pure hustler."

You could never keep track of Mostyn, Boysie pondered. He was supposed to have been out of the service for a long time, except for the Air Apparent thing. Slippery as a soaped streaker, that was Mostyn.

"And you're a body-maker."

"A discoverer as well."

"We're all that - all bodies just waiting to be discovered."

"Lyric Lavenham, home-spun philosophies to order."

Towards the end of the apricot tart, she said, "Bob once said you were more lady-killer than hit man. True or false?"

"Depends on the ladies. Besides, that was a long time ago. I've changed, and your brother didn't know me very well."

"It's getting late," Lyric looked at her watch. They had taken nearly two-and-a-half hours over dinner.

"Oh Jesus," it was a low and anxious moan.

"What?"

"Bloody Mostyn. He wanted me back in an hour."

"He frightens you, doesn't he?"

"Too right the little sod frightens me. Lyric, I have to go."

She gave a pout. "Will you be with him for long?"

"No idea." Boysie was making frantic motions towards the waiter and fumbling with a fistful of francs. "Why?"

"I thought we could have a drink. At my place. Coffee, if you like."

The world brightened. Wagner at his most strident played in Boysie's head and there was a large pyrotechnic display going on, making fast for the loins. It was the best invitation he had received in weeks. The Wagner turned into the theme from some super sloppy epic, all swooping strings and tremolos. "I'd love to do that. Can I just see what the little shi ... devil wants and then check back with you?"

"Great. I presume they have room service."

"If not, I'll stand in."

Boysie walked her back to her room. At the door she laid a hand lightly on his arm, reached up and kissed him on the corner of the mouth, whispering, "See you soon."

"Hallo," thought Boysie. For a second, he felt definitely old. "Quick as I can."

He knew that he was leering, but his step had a decided spring as he traced his way down the passage towards Mostyn's door. Just before reaching it, he did a little hopping dance step.

There was no immediate reply when he knocked, so he knocked again. Without warning the door jerked open, almost pulling Boysie inside.

The room was dim, only one lamp burning, but he could make out Mostyn by the window standing absolutely still. He did not recover his balance, a fist helping him forward and onto the floor.

Things seemed to be happening very slowly. He saw Mostyn move and heard him call, "Boysie, for Chrissake look ..."

As that was going on he was reaching for his hip pocket, but someone was holding his neck, another hand going for the hip pocket. Mostyn was catapulting across the room. The Baby Browning was out, but not in his hand. Then the loud explosions - two of them blanketing his right ear.

A second before, Mostyn had been leaping towards him, now the body was moving to the right, but with little motive force, as though he was crumpling. There was a thud as he hit the floor and rolled over. Then a jagged blind of pain behind Boysie's ear. He knew his right hand was clawing for something, and, through the dimness, he had found it, the butt of his Baby Browning. Then he heard, a long way off, a muffled curse and a door closing.

Shaking his head, Boysie found himself, still in semi-darkness, on his hands and knees, his gun clutched in his right hand, the smell of powder around him and the stinging ring, from the shots, in his ear. Shouts and a hammering on the door.

Then the lights came on and all hell broke loose as Couperose dragged him to his feet.

IX - SWAN SONG

Collection published after composer's death

To begin with, Boysie was convinced it was a con. Couperose was calling him names, the automatic had been ripped from his hand and the room seemed full of strange faces.

On the floor lay what looked like a pathetic bundle of clothes, only he recognised, all too well, the short grey tight curls on top of the head. The bundle of clothes was James George Mostyn, and the spreading pool around him was blood. That was no con, Boysie had seen blood too often before.

There were two men kneeling over Mostyn. They turned him onto his back and the head lolled to one side, mouth open. One of the men looked up at Couperose and shook his head.

"So you've killed him, like the others," Couperose said quietly.

"What d'you mean, killed? I didn't kill anybody. Anyway, that's Mostyn. You don't kill Mostyn."

He could not believe it, too much of his past was tied up with Mostyn, too many horrific moments, a lot of good things as well. Christ, who was there now if Mostyn had gone? It couldn't be.

But, in the confusion, Boysie began to perceive that it was so. That James George Mostyn, one time Second-in-Command of the Department of Special Security, was dead. The lolling grey face, looking its age now, was as lifeless as the eyes staring up from it.

He was in shock, that would be it. But why the handcuffs. That was something he could not comprehend.

"Look," his voice sounded strange. "Look, what the hell's wrong. Why ...?"

"Come on, Oakes. It's useless to bluff now. We caught you red-handed." Couperose seemed to be a mixture of smugness and anger, his accent more pronounced.

"Red-handed my arse. What?" Boysie tried to gesture. "Me? You must be out of your skull. Mostyn's been my control for years. Jesus, it's like losing one's ... I don't know how to ..."

"You hated his guts. You made no secret of that. Anyway, it's cut and dried."

"It's not bloody cut and dried." Boysie attempted to explain what had happened, but even he could hear how implausible it sounded. "There was someone else here when I knocked. Jesus, Couperose, I'd only just left Lyric. I've been with her all evening. I was late back and I was going to have coffee with her as soon as I'd seen Mostyn. I wouldn't be fool enough to start loosing off guns in here."

Couperose considered the matter for a second or two. "We shall see," he said enigmatically.

"Well, for crying out loud, get these bleeding things off." Boysie motioned with his hands.

There were some quite heavy French plainclothes men in the room and one of them began talking to Couperose. The Intelligence man let off a string of French which Boysie did not even try to follow. He could not take his eyes from what they were doing to Mostyn's corpse: wrapping it in plastic. He felt suddenly very sick and lonely. There was nobody, nothing, upon which he could vent his natural rage: no focal point for the blame, for the bad things that happened. He had never realised how dependent he was on the oily Mostyn. The late oily Mostyn.

The heavy French copper departed.

"We're checking on Lyric," said Couperose, the implication being that he was concerned for the girl's wellbeing: an attitude that began to irritate Boysie.

"Are you going to get these sodding bracelets off?"

Couperose gave an exaggerated shrug. "How can I?"

"Perhaps you could conjure up Houdini's shade to give me lessons. Just unlock the bloody things: I'm warning you, Gerard, much more of this pissing about and you're going to find yourself in the merde."

Couperose remained composed. "Just keep quiet and nothing drastic will happen to you."

They were putting Mostyn's body onto a stretcher. As one of the officers opened the door for its last exit, the plainclothes man returned, engaging Couperose in another Gallic flurry during which Couperose shot interested glances towards Boysie.

At last the chatter finished and Couperose came over. "It seems that Lyric bears out your story," he did not look entirely convinced. "She heard the shots only minutes after you left her. She also says that she heard someone running down the corridor." Reluctantly he was unlocking the cuffs. "This does not mean you will not be charged. You happen to be the prime suspect, and when my superior gets here you will be properly interrogated. You will keep yourself in readiness. You will go to your room - which we have searched - and remain there, under guard. There is much to do."

Boysie opened his mouth to complain and then shut it again. Tightly. There was no point in rousing further antagonism. He needed time to think.

Couperose motioned towards the door. Outside, a uniformed gendarme waited. Boysie went quietly down the corridor to his room, and the gendarme opened the door for him, closing it firmly once Boysie was inside. There was no sound of a key turning so Boysie dropped to his knees and squinted through the keyhole. The gendarme stood outside. Only a major disaster would budge that one.

He straightened up. There were too many lights on, even with the curtains closed. He still had the horrors of some unseen sniper potting at his shadow. Quickly he snapped off all the lights, leaving only the bathroom illuminated, the door open. He pulled a chair into the angle of the bathroom door for cover and sat down. Think logically, he told himself. If you think logically you'll find a way. His eyes strayed across the room resting on the telephone. Griffin. Of course, if he was back, Griffin would create a diversion. Keeping low and away from the window, he edged over to the bed and telephone.

There was no dialling tone, only a high-pitched whine. Couperose was also thinking logically.

Boysie tried to put himself in Couperose's position. It did not take long to come to conclusions about that. As far as Boysie was concerned, Couperose had him and a circumstantial case against him. If Couperose was master-minding the security he had failed miserably, and the Frenchman's first concern would be his own beefy neck. Boysie had marked Gerard Couperose as a heavy from the start: he would not care a two-penny belch about Boysie's neck.

So, what was the conclusion? The conclusion, Boysie, my lad, he told himself, is that you have got to get the hell out. Once out you will, possibly, draw the fire of whoever had the drop on the Puebla team. He did not let his mind linger on the question of drawing fire. If he allowed that, fear would swamp him. Get out, he thought. Run. But how, and to where?

If it was a television series he could feign illness: the gendarme would dash in, loosen his collar, and in a flash, Boysie would overpower him, change clothes and walk out calmly. But this was for real and Boysie knew, with horrible clarity, it would go wrong from the start if he tried that way. He could not tunnel out. It is almost impossible to tunnel your way out from the fifth floor of a Paris hotel. Start a fire? The way things were going he would get himself charred in the process. Hide and confuse them? He looked around vacantly. There was nowhere to hide-except perhaps the wardrobe where he might just do a passable impression of a suit. He would not fit in the chest of drawers. There was the bathroom and ... He stopped. There was a way. A connecting door between this and the next room, secured with a slide bolt on his side. Boysie thought about the layout for a moment. The door would lead straight into the room next to the one which Mostyn had occupied.

He went over and tried the slide bolt. It was obviously not often used and proved stiff. Eventually it gave and Boysie gingerly opened the door, peering into the adjoining room. It was empty, the bed made up, but no sign of habitation: no suitcases, no clothes.

He moved fast, grabbing his spare suit, the dark grey one he had bought with his first week's salary from SEAT, a clean shirt and tie from the wardrobe, changing behind the bathroom door.

He checked his pockets for passport, his British currency and the fifty pounds or so which he had in francs. He also slid his small leather-cased manicure set into the hip pocket of his trousers, shrugged on his overcoat and went over to the connecting door, gently eased it open again and slipped into the adjoining room.

Boysie closed the door behind him, sliding the bolt, duplicated on the empty side, into place. If they came into his room now there would be a few seconds' confusion before they worked out which way he had gone.

Now he had to get from this room, downstairs to the foyer and out into the streets. If he got that far, where then? Take it one step at a time, he told himself.

The gendarme who had put him into his own room would be only a few paces away if Boysie emerged from this one. But to the gendarme he was a man wearing a dark suit. Boysie now wore grey, and a collar and tie instead of the roll neck. What he needed was another face.

Sitting in front of the dressing table, Boysie took out his manicure set, removed the nail scissors and carefully cut a sizeable lock of hair from his thinning scalp.

Putting the set back into his pocket, he began to work at the tuft of hair, manipulating it until it became the passable shape of a drooping moustache.

On the dressing table there was the usual hotel folder containing sheets of notepaper, envelopes and postcards. Carefully moistening a finger, Boysie dabbed it onto the adhesive backing of one of the envelopes, transferring the now tacky gum to his upper lip. He did this half-a-dozen times, until the lip was unpleasantly sticky. Then he held the false moustache in place and pressed. After a few seconds the hair seemed to have set against the skin. He put on his sunglasses and looked at himself. It was Boysie Oakes in a false moustache and sunglasses. Unmistakable.

He frowned, picked up a few sheets of the flimsy notepaper, and stuffed them into his cheeks. It was now Boysie Oakes with a false moustache and padded cheeks, but the gendarme had not really got a good look at him. It was just audacious enough to work. If his nerve held. Strangely, for Boysie, his nerve was managing very well. He had to get out; if he stayed in semi-custody there would be no chance. He had to put himself in a position from whence he could get whoever had killed Mostyn - and, presumably, the others. He would not do that by sitting on his backside being humiliated by Couperose, or interrogated by the coppers.

He rose and took a long look at himself. It was still not quite right. The moustache tickled and the paper tasted odd in his mouth. He ruffled his hair and assumed a stoop. It might pass. The only way to find out was to go and try it.

Taking a deep breath, he opened the door and walked firmly into the corridor. The gendarme outside the next room hardly glanced at him. The remainder of the corridor was empty, except for a man at the lift.

He closed the door and went through a pretence of locking it before walking, in a somewhat shambling stooped gait, towards the lift.

The uniformed man at the end of the corridor looked at him with interest as he approached. Boysie merely nodded, passing the lift, turning to the right and going down the stairs.

There was a lot of activity in the foyer, but nobody stopped him, or even seemed to notice him. In a matter of minutes he was out on the pavement and making his way towards the Place Charles De Gaulle.

After half-a-dozen paces the moustache fell off.

***

Boysie felt a great deal safer once he reached the Champs Élysées. It was a mild night, the traffic was chocked solid and the pavements crowded. Tourists, as easily recognisable as tramps at a garden party, jostled with the evening strollers; men in shirtsleeves gesticulating deep in political argument; couples arm in arm who did the route every night; middle-aged lovers grasping for a final fling; executive white hunters in search of pleasure, and the buoyant young, bejeaned, T-shirted, or decked in their own particular fashions: unquenchable, immortal, though certainly not invisible.

The cafés were crowded - raked amphitheatres viewing the evening's ever-changing entertainment. Boysie spat out the paper from his mouth, depositing it in a litter bin, took off his glasses, wanted to nip into the nearest café for a quick double *fine*, thought better of it, and wondered where the hell he should go now.

A whore? Hardly. If the police really were going to hold him responsible for Mostyn's death, they would be asking the whores.

Then he remembered Zizi Portobello.

***

The hotel was in one of the many side streets behind the Opera. Chiliman knew it well enough for it had a small reputation: half-hotel, half-brothel.

The room was on the second floor, which pleased Chiliman. Stairs were becoming more difficult these days. He tapped at the door and there was some scrabbling from inside. He tapped again and Gest opened up.

He was naked except for a towel around his waist. A girl was lying on the bed, a sheet thrown over her.

"I wasn't expecting you." Gest opened the door wider and Chiliman entered. He could not take his eyes off the girl.

"Can we ...?"

"She's all right. She knows." Gest was irritated.

"Well, James?" wheezed Chiliman.

"There's been a balls."

"How?"

"Mostyn's dead, but the other had to be left. A bungle."

"Then it had better be unbungled, fast."

"They confined him to his room. I think they were going to nail him for it. But he's out: loose. There's just been a newsflash." The television flickered silently in a corner, the sound turned down.

Chiliman began to laugh. "That's rich, James. They were the last two. Only those two and it would have been finished."

"Well, there's only one now, and the police are looking for him."

"Then you'd better start looking as well. I want him dead, James. You fix it. I want him dead, quickly."

"He has to be found first; it'll take time."

"You get it done."

"I've got a rehearsal in the morning."

"I'm not talking about the morning. I want him found as from tonight. Where would you go if you were a lone Englishman on the run in Paris?"

"He must have contacts."

"Find out. I pay you and I expect results. I don't expect you to spend the night whoring."

"I didn't think time was important."

"It is now. Where would *you* run to?"

"A safe house."

"Quite, but where? We don't know what facilities he has. Would you try and make it back in his shoes?"

"No, not unless there was a special route primed for me. He's got too much running against him. If it was me I'd go for something outlandish, or something long out of my past - a safe house nobody knows: an old friend perhaps."

"Well then. There is an old friend. Let's hope he thinks the same way, but try to cover every contingency."

"I'll try. All hell will be breaking out in London I'd imagine. They'll be pulling all the stops out."

"And putting new ones in."

Chiliman smiled as though it was a luxury he could ill afford.

X - DESCANT

Additional part, sung (sometimes improvised) above a given melody

THE Minster's PPS called just after eight o'clock. The Minister wanted to see him immediately. It meant only one thing, and that worried William Edith. Mostyn was either incapacitated, had resigned, or was dead.

He dialled the Department number and asked for the Duty Officer, but he was not available. William Edith repeated his name, coming on heavy, but was again told, more firmly this time, that the Duty Officer was not free to take calls.

He thanked the operator in his soft quiet voice which emphasised the sibilants, went into his bathroom, washed his hands with great care, replacing the soap and nail brush with an exactitude which bordered on obsession.

Glancing in the mirror he felt the well-known reaction which always baulked his vanity. His face was too fleshy and, to him, the slightly twisted neck muscles always appeared exaggerated. He stayed looking for long enough to ensure that the long, springy and tightly curled hair was neat. Neatness was definitely an obsession.

There were few who liked William Edith, but he was not in a competition to be the most loved man in the world. He knew that he was disliked, and he did not care very much.

They did not like his manner, his particular brand of ruthlessness, wayward moodiness or occasional bursts of violent temper; neither did they care for his capacity for prolonged concentration, his single-mindedness, and overt ambitions. They also had stupid reasons for disliking him : his scrupulous memos, files, and organisation; his methodical tidiness and the way in which he dressed - the Ministry and the Department preferred conservative clothes. William Edith owned only one suit, had no taste regarding colour, and his build did not easily lend itself to elegance. Nobody liked senior officers who went around in roll necks or T-shirts and jeans.

William Edith appeared to many as a little man - he was only five foot six (five foot nine when he wore the ludicrous platform soles) and his many enemies felt that his pettiness was simply a reflection of his small stature. Outwardly, William Edith did not care; inwardly, in the most classified recesses of his mind, he knew there was some truth in the idea.

He was also mean and only used his spotless red mini when it was essential. Tonight he went by tube, taking the District Line from Hammersmith to Westminster, and walking the rest of the way.

The Minister wrinkled his nose when they showed Edith into his office - he had never forgotten their first interview, some three years before, when Edith had sported multi-coloured canvas shoes, a shoulder bag and a Mickey Mouse watch.

"We have a grave situation," he said, not daring to look up. "Colonel Mostyn was killed in Paris tonight."

"I'm sorry." Edith did not sound sorry.

"It means that your takeover will now have to be brought forward. Normally there would be no problem. DTS is a very small department these days, not like the old Department of Special Security, but it has inherited problems from the past."

"I'm aware of all that, Minister," there was nothing conciliatory about Edith's tone. "I have been an integral part of DTS since it was formed."

The Minister looked over his glasses. "Yes," he sounded uncertain, but then he had never been totally in favour of retaining the nucleus of the Department of Special Security to regroup into the Department of Tactical Security - an organisation small and mobile enough to be used for exceptional operations, or to act as a front for other Departments. There were too many problems from the past, too much inner wheeling and dealing, not to mention scheming. "Yes," he repeated, knowing that William Edith was one of the biggest scheming intrigue-masters in the entire service.

"Just give me the facts, Minister; and your instructions."

"You're to have full authority, Edith. You're to takeover and go straight into the field. You know about a man called Oakes?"

"I know all about Oakes."

"Did you know Mostyn had brought him in again?"

"Yes."

"How dangerous is he?"

"That shouldn't concern you, Minister. That's an internal problem. Why?"

"He's suspected of killing Mostyn."

Edith felt his back stiffen. "Oh?"

"Gerard Couperose put him under technical arrest."

"Idiot."

"And he escaped. It makes for a very tricky diplomatic situation."

"Have they hushed the Mostyn business?"

"His death?"

"Yes."

"No. Impossible. He was shot in his hotel room. There were Sûreté and Deuxième Bureau people all over. They've got a call out for Oakes now."

"Shit," said Edith with little passion.

"Quite, and now there are newsmen and television people crawling around. It'll even be on our news tonight."

"Top Civil Servant shot in Paris hotel? That sort of thing?"

"The only way to play it."

William Edith shrugged as though he wanted to pass responsibility to someone else.

"The Department have been briefed," said the Minister. "They're expecting you now, and arrangements have been made for you to go to Paris tonight."

"It's all a bit sudden."

"Death is like that." The Minister looked up over his glasses.

When he got outside, William Edith decided to walk to the DTS office. It would only take ten minutes and he needed that time to collect his thoughts. Despite his ambitions, William Edith had never intended matters to reach this stage. As he walked, his lips moved. Under his breath, he was using some very bad language. "Piss-piss-pissidy-piss," he chanted.

***

Zizi Portobello was really Griffin's friend; Boysie had first met her through the good offices of Griffin when on an assignment in Paris. They had remained firm friends ever since. In fact, Boysie thought now, as he headed for the Metro, in all probability Griffin was visiting her: he had said he was going to see a friend, and Zizi was the obvious choice.

He took the Metro to the Tuileries, for it was near there that the adorable Zizi was quartered in some splendour in a luxury apartment designed to cushion her from the harsher realities of living. She appeared to have a bottomless income which provided her with clothes from the most exclusive couturiers, a Bentley motorcar and many other things which made life just that little bit more pleasant.

Boysie had his theories about the source of her undisputed wealth, but he had never once even commented upon it. On leaving the Metro station he checked that nobody was tailing him, walking briskly to the block in which Zizi lived.

Her face lit up, breaking into a wide and unrestrainedly beautiful smile, as she opened the door to his ring.

"Boyzee," she screeched. "You are zee limit. I was just having thoughts about you."

"Good ones, I hope." Boysie stepped into the hall.

"No, Boyzee, thoughts of great worry. You 'ave been on zee - 'ow you say - zee pox?"

"The box," corrected Boysie, who was used to Zizi's particular brand of colloquial English - he well remembered her once, in a romantic mood, saying that they were "like shits that passed in the night". It was the only peculiar thing about her: age would not weary Zizi Portobello, nor would her special charm run out. From where Boysie stood, nothing had altered - the upturned nose with slightly flared nostrils, generous mouth and large brown eyes which always appeared to look upon the world with wonder.

His eyes traversed the rest of her. She was built on lines which had never known austerity. Whoever did the design knew all about pulchritude. It was also possible that, once built, they had thrown away the mould. Stunning was a corny word when used about Zizi Portobello; it was also underestimating the effect. This one was made to drive men wild and make others dissatisfied with their lot-even if their lot happened to be a combination of Raquel Welch, Bardot and Germaine Greer.

Boysie dragged his mind back from the obvious siding into which his natural sensuality was rapidly shunting him. It was a bumpy ride.

"They've had me on television?" he queried: part pride and part fear.

Zizi shrugged, gesturing him towards her living room. "Un'appily. The flicks are on your railroad ..."

"On my track."

"Your track, yes. Zey say as 'ow you 'ave done somebody up."

Boysie followed her, eyes doing a square search of the rounded buttocks, tight inside exceptionally well-cut jeans: if ever there were nursery slopes these were they.

"Mostyn," he breathed.

"Some Eenglish civilian waiter, zee television said."

"Civil Servant. They would call Mostyn a Civil Servant." Boysie reflected that there had been little either civil or servile about Mostyn.

"Zat ees what I said," Zizi pouted. "Yes, Moustin, zat was his name. Did you do 'im oop, Boyzee?"

"No. Can I have a drink?" He spotted the groaning liquor table by the window. There must have been the makings of a couple of hundred hangovers there.

" 'Elp yourself, I still have some champagne left. You are in zee soup, Boyzee."

"Up to my armpits," he separated several fluid ounces of Remy Martin from its bottle. "Charlie been to see you, Zizi?"

"Sharlie was 'ere tonight, Boyzee. 'Ee left before zee news on the pox."

"Box."

"But what am I to do for you, my darling? 'Ow can I 'elp you to make zee goaway?"

"First you call Charlie, at the Baltimore."

"I tell 'im you're 'ere?"

"Not straight out you don't. But you know Charlie well enough. You think you can let him know without actually telling him?"

"Simple. I can make zee insinuation. I am good with zee insinuations."

It took only two minutes. She dialled the Baltimore and asked for Griffin's room. A strange voice answered in French.

Boysie had his ear pressed to the receiver, bringing his head into close contact with Zizi. Her hair smelled like summer and long nights in secluded beach hotels, but this did not stop him from gesturing violently for her to cut the call.

She replaced the instrument and gave a nervous smile. "Zey will think I am a 'eavy bleeder."

"Breather. That was a flick, I wonder what's happened to Charlie."

"It ees not good," she returned to her chair, picking up the champagne glass once more. "Zey are going to be brushing zee city for you."

"Combing," corrected Boysie absent-mindedly.

"Eet's good to see you again, but I worry. You should not stay 'ere in Paris."

"They'll be watching the airports and stations."

"On the pox they were setting up road bricks."

"Blocks. Yes, they would."

She looked at him wide-eyed. "You remember my motor?"

"Your Bentley? Yes."

"There is no chauffeur."

"No?"

"But I still 'ave the uniform."

"He didn't get to keep it?"

"He kept little. Pity, 'ee was a beautiful boy, but I caught 'im 'ere," she pointed dramatically towards the carpet, "Making zee lovings to some poupee."

Boysie grinned.

"I make a scene. Pouf out they go into the street and no messes. 'Im without zee uniform and 'er without zee knickers. Zee uniform was expensive; zee knickers were cheap, from Uniprix: I consigned them to zee incinerator." She made an exasperated face and then exploded with mirth. "Eet was a big drama. Very satisfying. I 'ave not provided myself with a new chauffeur yet, but I think you would do well, Boyzee. Perhaps I wish to be driven down to zee South tomorrow, they will not be looking for a chauffeur on zee road bricks. You take zee job, yes?"

"If I get all the usual perks."

She came over to him, wrapping her arms around his neck. "Of course, my cherie, zee perks are always ready for you. We 'ave worked together in zee past."

She snuggled close, shifted into third and laid her lips over his. Boysie put her in fourth - with overdrive.

When they finally broke surface, Zizi sighed: all longing and edged with frustration. "I think you will fit zee uniform very well. But zat is for tomorrow. Tonight I 'ave to test your driving ability. I 'ope you 'ave not deteriorated since last time."

Boysie took in air; through his nostrils, deeply. "If anything, I think I've improved - old wine, good tunes on old fiddles and all that."

Her brow creased, "Wine? Fiddles? I am talking about zee 'umpings, darling."

"So am I. I meant that my cornering is better than it was, and I seem to be able to get more speed on the straight."

She looked at him for a long time. "It is good to see you again, Boyzee, but you are mad: all zee Eenglish are mad. You make me laugh, so tomorrow I get you out of Paris, and you get me out. Tonight ees for other things. I'm glad you came 'ere: tonight I am very abandoned."

Taking his hand, Zizi pulled Boysie to his feet and led him, unresisting, to her bedroom.

Paris slept. Many security and police officers did not. William Edith arrived and did not sleep. Neither did Boysie, nor Zizi.

XI - BREAK

A change in tone-quality encountered in passing between different registers

Mostyn's murder was still the lead story in all the papers, and the news bulletins carried it at number one. Zizi, sitting in the back of the Bentley wrapped in black mink, translated, in her own inimitable style, as the ORTF newsreader tripped and rolled the words over each other.

"Zere is still zee mystery going round zee death of an Eenglish civilian servant at zee Baltimore 'otel last night. Colonel James George Moustin, a tall-rank government official was shot dead in his chamber.

"Zee police have wishes to meet another Eenglishman who is fellow travelling with the corpse. 'Ee is Brian Oakes, tall with blue eyes and muscles. 'Ee is possibly dangerous and should be gone up to with cautions - I've always gone up to you with zee cautions, Boyzee.

"Zee police also search for another Eenglish couple, named Sharles Griffin and Lyric Lavenham, who were in Paris last night. 'Ee's describing Sharlie, Boyzee. What do they want with Sharlie? And who ees this Lyric Lavenham? She sounds like a cheap soap."

Boysie, sheltering behind sunglasses - in spite of the sky being grey as the chauffeur's uniform which he wore - felt concern inching up his spine. Griffin and Lyric were missing and that did not bode well. It did not bode anything at all.

"Why will they want Sharlie?" Zizi persisted.

"Maybe he stole the pea out of some passing gendarme's whistle," Boysie tried to be flippant. "Or spiked the Commissioner's Pernod."

"Be serious, Boyzee," for a second she sounded like the cutting edge of a commando dagger. "People 'ave died. You 'ave troubles. Now Sharlie 'ave troubles also."

"Sharlie always had troubles."

Zizi had gone out early and bought a few necessary things for him - razor and shaving cream, toothbrush and paste, two pairs of jeans, a jacket, three roll necks and four pairs of obscene underpants, the fronts of which were decorated with giraffes and elephants which took on extra dimensions when worn. Zizi was an extremely good judge of size.

They also laid careful plans. At any roadblocks she would explain that her chauffeur was suffering from laryngitis and could not speak.

Then, just before they left, she escorted Boysie down the street to the local Uniprix where he had his photograph taken on an automatic machine. Back in the apartment, Zizi disappeared for twenty minutes or so, returning with a Carte d'Identité giving Boysie's name as Jean-Baptiste Chênes. It looked like the real thing.

"Eet *is* the real thing, Boyzee," Zizi answered when he queried its source. "You think I would trifle with zee doggy merchandise?"

"The word is dodgy."

"Words," said Zizi with disdain. "Zee actions speak loudest."

It was also arranged, at Boysie's insistence that he would drive Zizi towards the Côte D'Azur, but would not take her all the way.

"It's good of you, and typical, but I don't want you too deeply involved."

Zizi looked pained, then shrugged her shoulders with Gallic fatalism. "We will drive to Chalon-sur-Saône, the Royal Hotel there is magnifique for the lovings. One night of blissfulls and then we part, just like zee lovers in a romance." She gave a small sigh; then her face broke into a dazzling and wicked smile. "Maybe I can get a new chauffeur on my way back to Paris."

She went to the door, then, as though changing her mind, retraced her footsteps into her living room, emerging a few moments later carrying a small black automatic pistol which looked as though it would be good for starting races.

"I've 'ad this for a long time," she offered the weapon to him. "It's good, yes?"

Boysie took it - a .22 calibre Beretta Jaguar with a full magazine, all eight shells, and a loaded spare. "It's good no," he grinned. "But better than nothing. With luck you might stop a mouse with it. You'd have to get very lucky to kill humans."

"Let's 'ope you don't 'ave to; but if you do, then you'll be lucky - I promise."

They headed out on Autoroute 6, negotiating two road-blocks manned by alert police who Zizi lulled into a sense of male chauvinist superiority by the judicious use of a throaty voice and bland sensuality. It was a performance which must have ranked among the greats - including Bernhardt's Phedre.

Both Boysie and Zizi chuckled happily as they sped away from the city's environs and the sun finally broke through the grey overcast.

Neither of them noticed the white Peugeot keeping station at a good distance.

The Nostradamus was not a clip joint, you only paid one hundred per cent more than in a respectable club, and that came pricey if you were taking the wife out for steak and chips; only you did not take the wife to a place like the Nostradamus: there was too much competition.

At nine in the morning the interior looked, and felt, as drab as an alcoholic's tongue. Gest had no wish to be there, but there was not much option. He had a contract, and that meant rehearsals were necessary. The rehearsal pianist was a big black heavy whose musical ear was not over accurate, and Gest was getting irritable when Maurice, one of the barmen, came through to say that he was wanted on the telephone.

The team had been searching for most of the night, and Gest was tired, having been up directing the operation by phone. They had been successful they thought.

Now Henri was calling him.

"We were right. He's there with the girl and they look as though they're moving out."

"How?" Gest sounded as though an ice cube would not even sweat on his lips.

"Car. She has a Bentley and it's been brought round."

"Okay. Stay with them. Complete it if they get clear."

"I'll come back to you."

"Do that."

He replaced the receiver, took it off again and dialled Chiliman's number.

"My team's onto them."

In his mind he saw the slim Henri and swarthy Michel together in the Peugeot. They were both professionals who could do a job well, with minimum fuss.

"Good," muttered Chiliman, breathing heavily. "Tell me when it's done and make it soon."

"It'll be in the open. Out of Paris. I have no control over time."

"Just do it." Chiliman put down the phone and Gest, feeling more irritable, stomped back into the main room of the club where the black pianist had put his instrument into idle.

***

They lunched at the Petite Auberge in Auxerre ignoring the covert glances from other patrons who did not approve of the blatant relationship between mistress and chauffeur. Zizi flirted outrageously through the Consommé Mercedes laced with sherry; Boysie returned the compliment during the Côtes de Veau à la Maraîchère, and the whole business became warmly erotic at the arrival of the Gateau Saint-Honoré, and, later, the cheese: Boysie crunching at the celery sticks in bad imitation of Albert Finney as Tom Jones, Zizi drinking her La Tache as though it was moisture from a lover, sipping and flicking her tongue into it in a manner which Boysie found disturbing enough to banish all caution. Death, his or anyone else's, was a million light years away and there was a power strike everywhere but in his loins.

They left Auxerre in a flush, drove a couple of miles, turned off into a side road, found a coppice with mossy banks which would have delighted Oberon or Titania, or both, stripped and took each other in a fury which dimmed the already weak sun. An hour later they were back on the road, this time abandoning the fast autoroute and taking the N6 down through Avallon and Saulieu to Chalon-sur-Saône.

They parked on the outskirts of the town, allowing Boysie to change from the formal grey of the chauffeur's uniform into the recently acquired jeans and turtleneck. At five-thirty they drove into Chalon, through the old coach entry of the Royal Hotel and into the parking lot behind. Stretching themselves like lazy cats, they strolled quietly into the hotel reception where they were welcomed with professional élan.

The room had leaded windows, panelled walls, a large bed and an atmosphere which merged solid dependability with a hint of romanticism.

Zizi flitted around, unpacking as though she was there for a long stay, while Boysie, tired from the recent exertions, stretched out on the bed, lulled by Zizi's mutterings and the few street sounds which filtered from below.

In this state he drifted into a half-sleep in which his subconscious took over, leading him into a dream fantasy in which he was a lozenge in a glass with a handful of other lozenges. It was safe and comforting, because he knew the lozenges were really people, like himself, who could be activated by the addition of a little water. But, at that moment, he hoped nobody would add the water. He liked being a lozenge.

If Boysie had been conscious of all the sounds going on around him, he might have identified the hum of the white Peugeot's engine as it passed the hotel; then, again, when it returned ten minutes later, swinging into the parking lot. Its two occupants got out, examined the Bentley, and made for reception to secure overnight accommodation.

Henri and Michel were relieved. They had lost track of the Bentley after leaving Auxerre, having no idea that their quarry would turn off merely to indulge natural appetites. For a few hours they wasted time, searching roads and stopping at numerous hotels to examine the cars in parking lots. Coming across the Bentley at The Royal, Chalon, had been a combination of luck and experienced thoroughness. Another hour and Henri would have been forced to call Gest in Paris and admit they had lost the scent.

Boysie's sleep curve began to descend, and with it the subconscious threw up basic insecurities. The safety of the lozenge dream dissolved. Instead, Boysie walked down some exclusive street, to a hairdresser where he left his head to have the hair cut. Then, suddenly, it was time to get to an appointment and he needed his head, but could find neither the street nor the hairdresser.

He was sweating when Zizi woke him, kissing him gently around the mouth and making soothing noises. Her eyes showed puzzlement and concern.

"You were making zee mooning noises."

"Moaning," Boysie automatically corrected. "What's the time?"

"Seven. Time to eat."

Boysie grinned at her, his face belying the trepidation and depression which had come with the dreams. "Do I get a choice of starters and dessert?"

"They 'ave a good menu."

"Potage à la Zizi and Strawberries Zizi."

She waggled a finger at him, "Do not laugh, Boyzee. There is such a dish as Strawberries Zizi."

"I know, I ate it after lunch."

"No, it was created in my honour by a prince."

"Royalty. I'm impressed."

"Well," she shrugged with a little moue. "He was only a White Russian prince, employed at Maxims at zee time, but Strawberries Zizi is inspired. You make it ..." "With strawberries?"

"With pineapple, scooped out and filled with zee berries and soaked in sugar and best champagne cognac."

"And you drink the gravy. Okay, Zizi, let's eat and get smashed in celebration of my escape. Then, in the morning you can drive me to Dijon where I'll catch a train for the south."

She laid a hand on his arm. "You sure I can't come with you, Boyzee?"

"Positive, fancy face. I have a feeling that even if the gendarmerie don't catch up with me, someone else will, and that I would not wish on my worst enemy."

Boysie washed, combed his thinning hair, slipped into the jacket which Zizi had purchased that morning, and, after a moment's hesitation, checked that the Beretta was loaded before sliding it into the right hand pocket.

They ate regally - coquilles de volailles, homard à la broche Ravigote, and sabayon à la Creole-and drank the best part of a magnum of Heidseck. Neither took any notice of their fellow diners - there were eight or nine other people in the dining room, including the two men who had booked into the hotel earlier that evening: this pair finished their meal and withdrew a good half-hour before Boysie and Zizi brought their dinner to its coffee and brandy conclusion.

"I am pickles," announced Zizi as they left the dining room.

"Good for you," Boysie's head was spinning pleasantly and the world looked decidedly rosy. "I think a breath of fresh air would do us no harm."

Zizi grinned stupidly. "We will go and wish Benjamin a good night."

"Benjamin?"

"My motorcar; my Bentley. I am always giving him a name. I call heem Benjamin. Benjamin Bentley."

"Since when?"

"Since about a minute ago. Boyzee, I love my motorcar. I must see he ees tucked in for zee night."

They strolled gently out to the car park, passing a Fiat and a little white Renault standing near the shadow of the hotel wall.

"Look," said Zizi, raising an arm dramatically, "Benjamin 'as company." There was a white Peugeot drawn up next to the Bentley. "I wonder if they are 'appy together."

"Maybe," started Boysie, slowly, "maybe in the morning there will be a new race of little super cars"

"Peugelies," laughed Zizi.

They picked out two more unsteady paces before Boysie's intuition reacted: he had a sudden mental picture of the Merc riding Mostyn, Couperose and himself into Paris from the airport, and the white Peugeot leeched to them along the motorway.

The short hairs on the back of his neck rose in unison with the flip roll of his stomach. In spite of his blood-alcohol level, Boysie moved with surprising speed, leaping away from Zizi, drawing the Beretta and flicking off the safety, crouching low and spinning full circle, at the same time shouting, "Get away, love. Get some cover. Behind your car." Simultaneously he wished he had some heavy armament - a Colt 45 or that Luger Mostyn had given to him in Mexico ten years before.

He did not actually sight the figure shadowed in the hotel wall, seeing only the flash and hearing the bullet hit something behind him - the Bentley possibly; but by this time his Beretta was up and he squeezed the trigger three times, pointing rather than aiming towards the flash.

For a couple of seconds his brain recorded only sounds: a short gasp from the shadows of the wall, a clatter and falling noise; Zizi's little shriek and the sound of her shoes as she ran towards the Bentley; then the other shot - a flash from near the Peugeot - the crack in his left ear merging with the thump and a shout, in French. He fired twice towards the cars and saw the shape of the gunman as he stood, perfectly still, full-frontal, taking careful aim.

Automatically Boysie ran towards the cars, firing twice more, wildly, at random and only in the general direction of the figure. The shot came, and again missed, Boysie's two rounds having thrown the man.

He yelled again, "Zizi, take care, you're going towards him."

But it was too late. Zizi came into his line of vision, close to the gunman who was now between the two cars. He saw the figures merge, heard Zizi shriek again and then heard the sickening slap of a bunched hand on flesh.

Boysie dived to his right, rolling as he went, back towards the Fiat and Renault, the concrete jarring his back and shoulders as he went. There were other sounds from the hotel, confused shouts and running.

From the area of the Peugeot and Bentley, the French voice roared out again. "Michel. Michel." Then the slam of a door and a hurried burst of life from the Peugeot's engine, lifting to a roar as the car suddenly came alive, surged in reverse, and then leaped forward, its headlights full on, heading for the exit.

Boysie lifted his right hand, squinting along the sights, but the hurried impression was of a man in the driving seat and a woman slumped next to him.

He seemed to have got lucky as Zizi had predicted, for there was no further sound from the darkness of the hotel wall, though activity escalated around the door leading from the hotel to the car park. Boysie's hand dipped back into his pocket, fingers coming into contact with the Bentley's keys which Zizi had left in his care. Dizzy and off-balance, he staggered to his feet, taking off at a sprint towards the car, aware that the Peugeot with the gunman and, presumably insensible, Zizi, had braked violently and was turning left out of the coach yard entrance.

There was no fumbling. The driver's door came open fast: the motor starting like a dream. It was only when Boysie was spinning the wheel to the left, streaking the big car out onto the road, that he realised he had not flicked the headlight switch.

XII - SOLO

A piece or passage performed by one person-either alone, or with others in a subordinate, accompanying role

Anger bunched the muscles on William Edith's neck and around his mouth. It was a livid anger as transparent as polished plate-glass, but not as smooth.

He had brought two young men with him to Paris. They stood, now, looking gloomy, their reflected moods rapidly alternating between reproach and apprehensiveness.

Gerard Couperose and two of his men in plainclothes, plus a uniformed officer, had the look of people in high dudgeon.

William Edith spoke softly, yet it was obvious to all that he was experiencing great difficulty in maintaining control.

"You're absolutely certain it was Oakes?" he said, menacing softly.

"It fits the description," Couperose began a shrug, then changed his mind. "He was registered as Jean-Baptiste Chênes. In French, chêne is ..."

"An oak. I know. I am conversant with your language. The woman was not Miss Lavenham?"

"There the description does not fit. No."

"The dead man?"

"Michel Pesant: a hoodlum, professional killer, known to us."

"He work with anyone in particular?"

Couperose looked towards the uniformed officer who passed the buck neatly back with his eyes. The glance indicated that the policeman's lot was not a happy one.

"It depends," said Couperose, this time steeling himself and actually shrugging.

"Depends on what?" Edith sounded lethal, like a cut-throat razor freshly stropped. "Depends on what?" he repeated. "His mood? Whether or not there's an R in the month? What are you running here, Couperose, a TV guessing game?"

"I resent ..." began Couperose.

"You resent?" Edith pulled himself up to his full height, which would have frightened someone of more stunted growth than himself. Yet there was unpleasantness in the action, "You have no right to resent anything. One of our senior officers has been murdered while under your protection. You are privy to facts. You know exactly what the circumstances are, and you cannot deny it." He threw a twisted leer across the room. "Mostyn was acting as a lure. I presume he had told Oakes."

Couperose hesitated. "I am not certain."

The pause went through pregnancy and ended still-born. Edith sighed. "That's Mostyn. But *you* knew all about it. You knew the set-up; you knew where the enquiries had led us. Yet you push Oakes around; lock him in his room, and then let him get away."

"There's a description out."

"Sod the description. The man'll feel hunted."

"I am perhaps not making myself clear. Oakes knew he was a lure. I'm not certain if he knew why or who was after him. Mr. Edith, I became uncertain. Oakes was in the room when the Colonel died. The bullets came from Oakes' gun. Oakes had it in his hand. It is possible that ..."

"That Oakes killed him? Don't be an idiot. With the information you had? Chiliman's in Paris, isn't he?"

"Yes, but ..."

"But you thought Oakes had got involved there?"

"It was a possibility."

"Don't be naive, Couperose. If he was involved, do you think Mostyn would not have known?"

"It was confused."

"And it's more confused now. Oakes is running from you and the police, and us, and the others. He does not know that only the others want him dead, and it's doubtful that he even knows why." He paused as though for effect. "Michel Pesant, deceased: with whom did he work?"

"Well, there is one man."

"Give."

"Henri Frelon."

Edith gave a snort. "Henry Hornet. His own name?"

"It's the name by which he's known. I don't think he was born with it."

"It sounds like something from Runyon," he heard the line buzzing in his head: 'I am stepping into Mindy's and who am I seeing propping up the bar but Harry the Hornet.' "Now the woman Oakes was with," he continued aloud. "We know anything there?"

"Nothing definite. If you untangle the statements, she seemed close to Oakes, and Frelon - if it is Frelon - abducted her."

"And Frelon is a dangerous customer."

Couperose wanted to say that Frelon was almost as dangerous as Edith. He simply nodded.

"And what of friend Griffin and the Lavenham girl?"

"Nothing."

"All in all, old lad," Edith precariously smooth, "you've made a right goulash. Mostyn dead; Oakes missing; Griffin missing! Lavenham missing and one hoodlum shot dead. Where, Couperose, do we bloody go from here?"

"We follow up on the Bentley."

"You think that'll do us any good? Find the Bentley and we find Oakes? Balls. Whatever else he is, Oakes is experienced. He's out of one trap. If I know his kind he'll dig in somewhere and wait for the news media to give him a clue about Pesant, or, possibly, Frelon. A clue that might lead him to the lady. You got any clues?" he needled.

"If it is Frelon, then he has a lot of contacts on the Côte D'Azur."

"That's more like it. Wait about," he scrutinised his watch, "about five hours. Then leak some juice to the Press. We know any of Frelon's haunts in the south?"

"Not off hand, but I can find out." Couperose moved towards the telephone like a greyhound who's spotted the electric hare a shave before any of his competitors.

Gest finished his second performance at ten thirty-six. It was a lousy house: a covey of American tourists and half-a-dozen French businessmen out on the make. The tourists lapped up the atmosphere; the French businessmen were too busy trying to grope their secretaries, or whoever was substituting for the wife, to take much notice of Gest's enunciation, breath control or self-assured handling of the lyrics.

The reluctant applause was raucous from the Americans and diffident from the locals.

Gest squeezed through the tiny passageway beside the bar, and went down the stairs to the small dressing-room which he shared with two members of the band. The band was still up there providing slow and lethargic music which would not overtax the clientele who were mostly of an age when shuffling close on a tiny floor was more attractive than leaping about in abstract frenzy.

Castervermentes was in the dressing-room picking his teeth.

"They've shredded it," he said.

Gest closed the door behind him, very quietly. He felt very tired and disillusioned. Two major blunders in forty-eight hours was as near disaster as you could get without actually bursting into flames.

"How?"

"I don't know the details. Michel got himself wasted."

"Dead?"

"Terminated," Castervermentes showed his gold fillings. "A small calibre slug right in the throat. Nobody got to him in time."

"Where did it happen?"

"Chalon-sur-Saône. There are further complications. Henri had to take the girl as a hostage. He called me. I haven't told Chiliman yet."

"And Oakes?"

"Disappeared, but he'll have to come up for air sometime. I told Henri to get the girl down to Cap Martin. To the house."

"Will Chiliman mind that?"

"He won't have to mind; and as for you, James, I suggest that tonight you are taken ill with the flu. I will deal with the situation here, but you should not appear for a couple of nights."

Gest nodded. "I should ...?"

"We should," Castervermentes sneered. "We should take an active part now. This has to be cleared up once and for all. Call Chiliman. Tell him what I have told you. Tomorrow I'll settle this place and make sure they have a replacement. Then we'll go down and join Henri. The woman must know his plans and she must share them with US."

Gest's face contorted fractionally-a wince, as though he was feeling some pain meted out to another.

***

Boysie was certain that the Peugeot had either taken the N9 out of Chalon, or crossed onto Autoroute 6. Certainly they were heading south, but after only fifteen minutes travelling Boysie knew the chase was impossible. The shoot-out at Chalon would have escalated matters and the police were after him anyway. They would soon have all the roads blocked and every mobile in the area alerted. One thing was sure: he had to ditch the Bentley soon.

He doubled back off the N6, pointing himself towards Dijon, peering through the gloom and taking stock. His natural instinct urged him to go on chasing, but his training and experience said something entirely different. There was little he could do to help Zizi or himself at this point. Hole up. Hole up somewhere quiet and wait for matters to break. The French coppers would be looking for the Peugeot as well as the Bentley. When something broke it would be all over the papers and TV.

It took only a few seconds for Boysie to make up his mind. Dijon was on the direct rail route to the south. He would never get as far as Dijon in the car, but that had to be his stopping-off point.

He drew the car into a layby and studied the map under the shaded interior lamps, conscious of the sweep hand of his watch pushing time on its way and narrowing the chances. He had come off the N6 onto a side road which had taken him through the village of St. Germain-du-Plain. If he doubled back in a wide sweep he could probably get to a point somewhere just outside Beaune, or even better make the wider sweep to Dole which was further east but appeared to provide more cover.

He snapped the lights off, restarted the engine and pulled out once more. There was little traffic on the secondary roads and Boysie sneaked the Bentley through the rough lanes with no trouble. An hour later he pulled the car off the road again, a few hundred yards from a signpost which told him it was four kilometres to Dole.

Sitting in the driving seat he pondered for the best part of a minute. Leaving the car there, in full view by the roadside, would be like chalking Indian signs. After all, a Bentley was not exactly standard transport for the area, and nobody was going to mistake it for a farm implement.

Slowly, Boysie got out and, standing in the shadow of some bushes, relieved himself, willing his eyesight to penetrate the darkness. Nothing, except the thicket of bushes which appeared to stretch back for ever.

Returning to the car, he manoeuvred it into position, then began to drive slowly and resolutely into the foliage. Above the engine note there was the crunch and slap of branches, parting whipping back against the windshield. After twenty yards the bushes proved too much even for the Bentley.

The car lurched, tipped to one side, the engine stalling. Boysie switched off the ignition, checked that the doors were locked, that the pistol was still snug in his pocket, then, taking a small torch from the glove compartment and stuffing the map into his waistband, he clambered from the car, closing and locking the door on the driver's side.

It was impossible to see how well the vehicle was hidden from the road, but he retraced the path the Bentley had swathed through the thicket, picking his way with the aid of the torch and, where he could, pulling the flattened bushes and foliage back into place until he once more reached the road. The whole operation took half-an-hour. Somewhere in the night an owl hooted and the sound of a car grinding its gears floated over the flat earth.

He stood still for a few moments, ears pricked and senses alert, aware that pinpoints of light clustered far away to his right, of the silent country sounds of the night, and an overwhelming sense of hostility. For the first time since the shoot-out he realised how frightened he was. But that was an old sensation, almost friendly now. If it told him nothing else, at least he knew through it that he was alive.

Almost casually, Boysie lit a cigarette, cupping his hand to hide the flame and drawing the poison deep into his lungs. Then, superstitiously, he crossed his fingers, hunched his shoulders against the chill night air, and headed towards the town, trying to push the next problem out of his consciousness.

Dole is an agricultural centre and particularly concerned with wine-in the Middle Ages it was part of Burgundy: its railway station has no sparkle, the bouquet is diverse, spicuous as a kangaroo in a cats' home. Public places are all little limbos and only fascinating to train freaks. Late at night even freaks would be put off by the ambiance of this station.

Boysie waited thirty-five minutes for a local and got into Dijon just after midnight. There he felt as conspicuous as a kangaroo in a cats' home. Public places are all dangerous if you're on the run - particularly at night when there are no crowds for cover. As he walked across the broad concourse at Dijon, Boysie felt vulnerable and not a little lonely -

as though somewhere out of sight a marksman had him firmly in the crossed wires of his scope.

Outside the station, in the streets, the traffic was sparse and there appeared to be few people on the pavements. Dijon was not exactly your swinging city, thought Boysie, even if the girls were supposed to be mustard.

Long ago, a hundred years it seemed now, in the army, Boysie had learned at least one useful lesson. If you are dodging the column, or are somewhere that you should not be, then the trick was to look as though you belonged and proceed with purpose. Now he set off down the street as if he was receiving the freedom of the city.

Hole up, he had said to himself; hole up and wait for something to break. The query came back loud and clear -hole up where? And how?

The French fuzz, he realised, had him both ways. He could not walk into an hotel and present himself as Brian Oakes, boy wonder, because they knew about Brian Oakes from Paris. Nor could he walk in with the Carte d'Identité claiming himself as Jean-Baptiste Chênes, Gallic garcon. They knew about Jean-Baptiste Chênes from Chalon.

How then would he hole up? A whore? Not the best way, he had decided that in Paris. A pick-up, male or female? Sweaty, and could prove difficult. The gloom began to settle as he pounded one leg in front of the other, not daring to syphon himself off into one of the many Bar-Tabacs which still seemed to be open.

It was dark, lonely and cold on the streets of Dijon. It was getting colder all the time and the street was no place to make friends, Boysie thought. Friends appeared to be getting more scarce with every step.

The Hotel Cloche hove in sight, placed opulently in what some would term a select commercial square: the sign said Place Darcy. It was big with a lot of lights. Most inviting, and Boysie kept heading towards it. He had read Arthur Hailey's *Hotel* like everyone else, and in that book there were a dozen wrinkles, fool-proof plans and tricks which got you into a hotel for free.

He reached the main doors and peeled off away from the hotel, knowing, with brilliant inner comprehension, that if he tried to emulate any of Arthur Hailey's characters he would fail miserably and end up in the hoosgow.

He circled the block, sniffing the air. The aroma around the Hotel Cloche was one of tranquillity, service, soft mattresses and cosseting. He needed cosseting, and from that need sprang nerve and action. After all, he thought as he climbed the steps, nerve was part of the job-the fact that his had always been shaky, except with women, was beside the point.

There was a tall young man with slick plastic hair behind the reception desk. He regarded Boysie as though he had inadvertently stepped into a careless pile of ordure. Boysie did not flinch.

"You speak English?" he snapped, trying to sound confident, authoritative and rather at the end of his tether.

The young man hesitated for a second. "Yes," he said with diffidence.

"My car has broken down, I've had to walk into Dijon, about three miles. I'm cold, dirty, I've just spent an hour with the garage and I want a room - your best if possible, with a bath."

It worked. The young man could recognise the voice of authority and money.

"Certainly, monsieur," his fingers clicked and a page materialised out of thin air. The other hand slid a registration card in front of Boysie. "Your baggage, monsieur?"

"It's in the bloody car. At the garage. I'll have it brought over in the morning. All I want to do is sleep now."

The young man looked doubtful for a moment, so Boysie dug into his pocket and brought out the French currency and traveller's cheques, praying silently. The young man held up a horrified hand, so Boysie put the money back and began to fill in the form.

Nom it said. Then, *Prenoms*. Boysie took no notice of that: forms were not for English milords. *Sir Richard Hannay*, he wrote. He gave his address as *Munching House*, *Gonad Place*, *London*, *W.8*. They also wanted his passport number so he scribbled 38765, added the date, signed the card and pushed it back at the receptionist.

"Your passport, sir?"

"Jesus Christ," Boysie exploded. "What do you want, my blood? The blasted passport's with my luggage - with the Rolls ..."

The receptionist picked up the passing reference to the Rolls with lifting eyebrows and glanced at the card. The *Sir Richard Hannay* did it. The superiority vanished, servility taking over and five minutes later Boysie was lying in a hot bath. Through the open doorway he could see a large bed; breakfast was ordered for eight in the morning with *Le Monde*, a razor and shaving cream. Boysie thanked heaven for the lingering class-consciousness of the classless society.

He dried himself, stretched, performed a couple of exercises without much enthusiasm, reloaded the automatic with the spare magazine and tucked it under his pillow, slid into the bed and allowed fatigue to take over.

He did not dream.

***

At five past eight a waiter woke him and there was a breakfast table laid out with a neatly folded paper next to his plate.

Boysie poured himself a cup of black coffee, broke a roll into two, spread it with butter and apricot jam, peeped into the bathroom to make certain the shaving gear had been provided, and sat down, stark naked, at the table. Even then he paused to take a sip of coffee, before opening the newspaper. Casually he unfolded *Le Monde* and there was no need to be a language expert in order to translate what he saw. Dry ice flooded Boysie's veins.

There was a large, and unflattering, photograph of himself on the front page. There was also a picture of Zizi, and of a man he did not recognise, though the text told him that it was Henri Frelon and the coppers wanted to interview him-badly.

At the bottom of the page there were a couple of inset maps: one of the area around Chalon with the Hotel Royal circled; another of the Côte D'Azur, from Cannes to Menton and the Italian frontier.

Don't panic, Boysie told himself, knocking over the coffee and making a dash for the bathroom. Just keep your head, the receptionist who had booked him in last night could well have gone off duty without seeing the paper. Anyway the photograph was not much good and you would have to be blessed with ESP to recognise Boysie. He ducked into the roll neck, back to front. There was something about it being unlucky to change clothing if you put it on the wrong way round. To hell with that. His hands were quivering as though the wrists were on springs.

Even when he was finally clothed, Boysie realised he was suffering from blasts of indecision. He needed a shave, but could not make up his mind whether to take the shaving cream as well as the razor-space in his pockets being limited. It seemed an age before he decided to jettison the cream, which was as well, for his pockets were already crammed with torch, pistol, passport and identity card, map, money and razor.

As a final gesture of good faith, Boysie leafed through his money, extracting some of the English bank notes which he threw carelessly onto the table. Leaving his key in the room side of the lock, Boysie departed.

No trouble in the foyer. No problems in the street either, except for an overwhelming desire to run. His stomach did one of its fancy spins as a police car whizzed through the Place Darcy. But it was followed by an ambulance, and preoccupied with matters far removed from Oakes. He reached the station a little before nine.

There was a train due in about seven minutes which would get him as far as Lyons. Otherwise it meant waiting until after ten when the 5025 arrived on its long run from Paris down to Nice. It would not be in his interest to hang about on Dijon station: that was as obvious as a harlot's mince. He would let the Paris-Nice catch up with him at Lyons. Boysie bought a ticket and boarded the train as soon as it came sliding to a halt.

He was ten minutes out by the time he realised that it was the wrong train. A local shuttle which would never arrive at Lyons. Feeling like a trapped goldfish, Boysie sweated it out, changed trains, backtracked and finally caught up with himself. His nerves were jangling and he thought he could feel the hot breath of invisible pursuers on his neck by the time he was eventually deposited at Lyons (Perrache).

The station at Lyons was like most other stations, though they did a better ham roll there than at Paddington. You could also buy litre bottles of red plonk from an elderly man who pushed a little cart up and down the platform. When Lyons finally caught up with the 5025 Boysie was in much better heart.

The train was not crowded and Boysie got a window seat in a compartment which contained only a young widow in black and a fat Italian lady with a small baby. Boysie thought it would have looked churlish to move when the baby started to cry just after they left the station. The baby was presumably crying in Italian. It was as rough as any other language.

Four compartments up, in the same carriage, Chiliman, Castervermentes and James Gest dozed. None of them had caught much sleep during the night, and the train left Paris at twenty to eight that morning. They knew that rest was essential. The next couple of days could be strenuous.

XIII - LEADER

The directing member of an ensemble

It was midday when Couperose brought the news in to William Edith.

"He spent last night at La Cloche, Dijon."

The Frenchman looked as though he had discovered the elixir of eternal youth.

"And you've got him," Edith leered unpleasantly.

"Unfortunately, no."

"Why not?" The words twin stilettos whispering into Couperose's brain.

"It was difficult. He managed to book in late, without showing a passport. Only two people saw him: a receptionist and a page. He signed in as Sir Richard Hannay."

Edith did not find it amusing. "He would," the voice soft as plastic explosive. "So where is he now?"

"He went to Lyons. He could have gone on from there heading south."

Edith looked up at him, slyly, his mouth smug and the eyes gleaming like those of a predator on the verge of a kill.

"Details," he demanded.

"He could have picked up the morning from Paris to Nice. I've got a man boarding at Avignon."

"You mean the 5025?" Edith prided himself for being well clued in.

"Yes."

Edith nodded. "Your man in Avignon, what are his instructions?"

"To mark him."

"I hope that's all he does."

Couperose detected that Edith knew more than he had divulged. "Why? The man is wanted. You want him, we want him ..."

"And the others want him: our friend Chiliman."

"Yes."

"Chiliman's on that train. It's the first time we have had a concrete tie between him and the man Castervermentes and our singing friend." Edith leaned back, savouring Couperose's puzzled expression.

"So."

"They're on the train with him."

Couperose gave a startled exhalation, eyes widening ... "Then we can perhaps ..."

"Then we can, perhaps, do nothing but watch. What time does your man get on that train?"

"It's due into Avignon at about quarter to two."

"Then get to him, Couperose. Get to him and cool him. I don't want fireworks or carnivals. When you've done that, get us on to the first flight to Nice."

"Us?"

"You. Myself, and one man each. We'll pick up Oakes in due course, unless he indulges in heroics. To be honest I'm more interested in Chiliman and Co. than in Oakes. Men like Oakes are two a penny. But Chiliman, well it's been a long haul drawing level with him: a long time and a lot of lives. One more isn't going to break the bank." William Edith was nothing if not ruthless.

Couperose showed no sign of emotion, even if he felt any, which was unlikely. "Nothing else?" There was no direct evidence that Couperose was being sarcastic.

"Not unless there's something new on Griffin and the Lavenham girl."

Couperose shook his head. "Nothing."

"Gone, like money in a drunk's pocket. That makes me nervous."

The telephone began to get agitated. It was for Couperose who conducted a quiet conversation with whoever was at the other end.

"Dijon," he said cryptically once the call had finished. "And?"

"The hotel room where Oakes stayed last night. They found a Beretta magazine with one round left in it. A little .22: a Jaguar, I think. Not much doubt that Oakes killed the man at Chalon."

Edith lifted an eyebrow. "What do you think I should do about it? Give the man a goldfish?"

"I'll get on to our Avignon man and see about our tickets."

"Do that," William Edith returned to his paperwork with the concentration of a Victorian spinster attacking her needlepoint.

***

There did not seem to be much dancing going on at Avignon, on or off the legendary bridge where it was supposed to happen. In any case Avignon was surrounded in a rosy glow as far as Boysie was concerned. The bottle, bought at Lyons, was empty and a second, purchased on the train, had been well pilfered. He was heading towards the Côte D'Azur and that thought blotted all the dangers from his, now slightly-overlaid, consciousness. The Côte D'Azur had once been one of Boysie's major stamping grounds and he had a lot of memory tied up in it. There were days and nights spent along that expensive strip of seaboard that he would carry with him for ever: there were also some scars.

As the train pushed on towards Marseilles through the afternoon, Boysie did that mental acrobatic trick which is so easy to fantasy-life players of his calibre: the past few days and the crowded events of the last years slowly faded away and he assumed the role of a tourist, a man most likely to, a prospective breaker of the bank at Monte Carlo, a lotus-eater willing to lap up the cream and spicy dressing which garnished a hundred willing and bronzed female bodies ever available on the beaches of Cannes, Antibes, Nice, Beaulieu, or decorating the lounges and bars of the Carlton, Negresco or La Reserve.

The strain melted and, by the time the train was twisting along the coast, through St. Raphael and Cannes, Boysie's smile had become set, his body relaxed. His ticket took him as far as Nice, though he had no exact plan, little idea of what he would do next. Nice had become a goal, a star, a stepping stone to the next unforeseen, uncertain, muddled move.

The train pulled into Nice (Ville) at twenty minutes past five and Boysie alighted, sniffing the air, still a little drunk, and grinning foolishly.

The sun was warm for the time of the year, for summer and the blazing heat was yet a month or two off, but the few people waiting to board the train were dressed casually, almost indiscriminately. Boysie joined the throng filtering out into the concourse and through the exits.

"Oakes," the voice was soft and came from a black Merc pulled up at the passenger loading and unloading point. The door was open and the man who had spoken leaned back in the front passenger seat: a young man, small with a slightly effeminate and twisted face.

Boysie whipped to his left, the right hand going for the Beretta. But the load of alcohol acted as a brake and before the hand was even halfway there, he spotted Couperose three paces to his right. Couperose had a Browning in his hand and a nasty look on his face. The combination persuaded Boysie that a shoot-out would not be in the best of taste, particularly for his mortal body.

"Okay," he tried a sheepish grin, "you've got me. But I didn't fade Mostyn."

"We know that," Couperose was motioning him towards the car, the gun now back in his pocket. "Please get in, we don't want people staring."

Boysie slid into the rear seat where a French heavy was already lounging in the corner. He recognised the man at the wheel from somewhere. Couperose came in behind Boysie and closed the door while the small young man in front twisted in his seat.

"We haven't met," the quiet voice greasy as butter. "My name's Edith."

"Lucky for you," Boysie grinned. Inside he did not grin. Inside he felt as though his stomach had become dislodged. He had seen Edith before, twice, flitting in and out of Shooter & Crump, and he could hear Mostyn's voice commenting, "Being groomed for stardom, that one. Little bastard, Boysie, keep clear of him. Beware men who are long on ambition and short on talent, they can never follow through."

"William Edith, Oakes, William Edith. Since Colonel Mostyn's death, I have been in charge of DTS."

"Nice for you," Boysie reflected that he could, if pressed, grow to dislike this one as much as he had loathed Mostyn. "What's DTS?"

Edith spoke to the driver. "Straight back to the hotel," then he turned back to Boysie. "The Department of Tactical Security, the natural successor to the old Special Security."

"I see. I was in Special Security."

Edith smiled: unctuously. "I do know, Oakesie," the inflection in his voice was uncannily like Mostyn's. Perhaps, thought Boysie, he was one of Mostyn's bastard children. The little devil must have had a dozen or so scattered around. "You are also in DTS," continued Edith as the car drew away.

"Ah," Boysie allowed the news to filter through. "Can you prove it?"

"Unfortunately for you, yes. You signed up again for poor old Mostyn."

"Ah," Boysie looked absently out of the window. "I resign."

"You remember the rules about resigning from the Special Security days?"

"Yes. You either die or you're pensioned off. I was sort of pensioned off when the Department packed up."

"Well, you got yourself pensioned back in again. You work for me now. I want you to tell me, first, who the woman was, whether you've any news of friend Griffin and the Lavenham girl, and everything that happened at Chalon."

"How about the winner of the 3.30 at Doncaster?"

"Oakes," Edith snarled, "when I want you to be funny I will give you advance warning, in triplicate. At the moment we're not here for the laughs, we're here, as you well know, to bring a costly and abortive operation to a close ..."

"Hold hard," said Boysie, his face colouring, voice rising, "just hold bloody hard, Mr. pouf-name Edith. All I know about this abortive operation is that Mostyn and I were bloody targets and Mostyn got chopped. I nearly got chopped. You? You're a lad, a fresh-faced puny lad who hasn't had enough time in the service to get his knees brown or his bloody number dry. I've been shot at and I object."

"I've read your file, Oakes," Edith looked grimly furious. "From that I often wondered about your intestinal fortitude."

"That does it," Boysie puffed. "I want out."

The Merc pulled up at the Negresco where the oddly-garbed commissionaire bent to open the door.

"Oh," Boysie deflated, "are we staying here'?"

"You listen to me, Oakes, and you listen good." William Edith showed his teeth which were disgustingly white. "The only way you will go out is in a box. You get that?"

Boysie hesitated for a second, trying to reckon up his chances. He decided the dice were loaded, the cards marked, and the odds heavily stacked against him. He tried the sheepish grin again.

"To hear is to obey, O master," he chanted.

They were installed in two suites and a couple of extra bedrooms on the fourth floor with a view out over the Promenade des Anglais. It was now late afternoon. William Edith's group ranged itself around the main sitting room, waiting for Boysie to start explanations. From outside, over the sea, there came a sound like an amplified angry roaring of bees. It distracted Boysie who moved across to the balcony.

Low over the sea three elderly biplanes were chugging through the air as though held up by wires.

"British Airways again," Boysie watched them, fascinated.

"It's an air circus," Edith irritated at the distraction. "They're putting on shows twice daily from the airport."

The English heavy had moved over to Boysie's side. "Nieuport Seventeens," he growled, obviously a World War One buff.

Behind the lumbering Nieuports came a little high wing monoplane, squat with a radial engine grumbling like an exhausted lawnmower, the fuselage strangely patterned.

"A Fokker," said the English heavy.

"Do you mind? The patchwork baron, I presume."

"I saw them last year at Perpignan. They give a good show, there was an RE 8 with them then, gave a demonstration of firepower with live ammunition." His hand came up, "There he is."

The odd and angular twin-seater biplane was making a long sweeping turn to come in behind the other four aircraft. Boysie could see the pilot and gunner, in the rear cockpit, clearly outlined against the evening sky.

"Jesus, they really fought in those things. A heavy rainstorm would knock them out of the sky," Boysie narrowed his lids and for a second he was Captain Oakes, Royal Flying Corps, watching his squadron coming in over the mud and rough huts after duelling with Von Richthoven.

"Oakes," Edith whispered, "if you don't come back in here and give me your full attention, I shall personally take you to the airport, tie you to the tail plane of one of those crumbling wrecks, tow you into the sky and drop you from a great height. Now: the girl, your escape, and Chalon."

Boysie slumped into a chair, the sound of the ancient aircraft receding. Quietly he told almost all that had happened since his escape from the Baltimore. Edith listened intently, asking no questions until he had finished.

"You have no idea who got Mostyn?"

Boysie shook his head. "I saw nobody."

Edith leered. "Think about it, Boysie boy. There's only one contestant."

Boysie thought: a desert, wasteland, Arctic snows. Nothing of any moment, except the desire to know what it was all about. That last thought turned into words.

"Why?" he asked, "why in all reason did somebody chop Mostyn? And what is it really all about? I know the Mexico operation in '64, has something to do with it. But what?"

"You've really no idea, have you?" William Edith's face became composed, almost friendly for a moment. "All right, Oakesie. Are you sitting comfortably? Then I'll begin."

XIV - CANTILLATION

Unaccompanied chanting in free rhythm - particularly in Jewish liturgy

It was a long and complex story which had its roots in the concentration camps of Hitler's Germany.

"How much did you know about friends Pinkney and Defoe?" asked Edith.

"Not much. They worked out of Paris. Whatever their importance it was carried in their heads. They ran to a freelance called Chiliman. The French and Americans wanted them alive. Mostyn wanted them dead. They got dead."

"You know about Clambake?"

"I knew they were working on it, but nobody gave me details."

Edith sighed. "Well, Clambake was Mostyn's own pet operation. Literally his own. He wanted to corner a certain market and he nearly made it."

"What market?"

"The most important Nazi war criminals still at large."

"Bormann ...?"

"Two in particular. Bormann and Mengele-the Doctor of Auschwitz."

Boysie raised his eyebrows.

"Pinkney and Defoe," Edith continued, "worked technically under joint NATO control. In fact they were Mostyn's operators. He had them, you might say, on a retainer. Their job was sensitive; the correlation of all information regarding the whereabouts of wanted Nazis: snippets, facts, hints, documents, statements, photographs. They sat in a room in Paris and sifted the lot. One might say that those two knew more about the movements of wanted war criminals than anyone else in Europe - probably more than they even knew at the Documentation Centre. And their most important conclusions were carried in their heads."

"Walking dynamite."

"Which blew them to pieces in the end. Mostyn wanted glory, Oakes. He wanted to nab the baddies single-handed."

"So did a lot of other people."

"They did indeed. The French, the Americans, the Russians, not to mention freelance operators. They were all getting edgy in '64 because time was running out. The Statute of Limitations was about to be brought into play."

"The charges would be dropped."

"For ever. Everybody wanted to get to them before that happened, and Pinkney and Defoe knew where both Mengele and Bormann were holed up in Argentina. They were also probably the only people who knew Mostyn's plan. Clambake."

"Which was?"

Edith shrugged, "Nobody knows now, not for sure. I suspect he was going to lift them, or have them liquidated pretty publicly. You would have been the boy to do that."

Boysie's stomach flipped.

"Then someone else got to them," Edith paused. "Caesar Chiliman who appeared to be a freelance working for the opposition. They were blown early and it must have given Mostyn a shock. The French and Americans knew how sensitive Pinkney and Defoe were and started to panic. I'll say that for Mostyn, he did remain cool. But friend Chiliman still had the edge, because he was not what he seemed."

"Not a freelance?"

Edith gave a negative shake of his head. "To use criminal parlance, Chiliman was Bormann's minder; and Mengele's. We'll never know how he got on to Pinkney and Defoe, but he did and he wanted them tucked away. The inducement must have been very large and they did not stand a chance. If Mostyn had not got them, then Chiliman would."

"He did."

"We know that now. Mostyn didn't know it for some time. Chiliman worked with an Argentinian called Castervermentes. Mostyn discovered that quite quickly and I don't think there's much doubt that Castervermentes pulled the trigger on Pinkney and Defoe. But the whole thing threw Bormann and Mengele. They had a lot of friends and nobody was very keen on Chiliman after that; him having let people get that close. He went into hiding and eventually carried on with the freelancing cover he had set up in order to get Pinkney and Defoe. Castervermentes became a showbiz agent."

"And they all didn't live happily ever after."

"Last year the past crept up on everybody. Mostyn was still searching. Chiliman knew the names of everyone involved and he'd kept out of their way. Until last year, in New York. He was spotted by Joan Palmer."

"And he spotted her."

"Fatally. They all just happened to be in New York at the same time. Castervermentes is agenting a singer called James Gest ..."

"I've seen him."

"Well, he's often broke and has a lot of underworld contacts : not averse to making the odd bit of loot on the side. Don't ask me what Chiliman's motivation is, but he is obsessed with wiping out everyone concerned with the 1964 Mexican operation." Edith smiled, lopsidedly. "And you're the last on his list, Oakes."

The telephone made them all jump. Couperose answered, conducting a rapid conversation in which he appeared to be asking a lot of questions and getting answers on the volley.

"They got off at Cap Martin," he told Edith after the chat was finished. "Car to meet them. They're at the Villa Veronique now. We can presume Mlle. Portobello is there also ..."

"With Harry the Hornet," mused Edith.

Couperose nodded.

"Can anyone join in?" from Boysie.

Edith grinned, "You did not know it, but you had company on the train. The terrible trio-Chiliman, Castervermentes and Gest."

"On the train?" Boysie swallowed.

"You're a lucky lad, Boysie. If they'd spotted you, it would have been the silk shroud."

Boysie thought for a moment. "Who's Harry the Hornet?"

"Henri Frelon. The heavy who abducted your girlfriend."

"And tried to fade me?"

"The same."

"And they're all here, with Zizi?"

"At Cap Martin. We knew Frelon had access to a villa down here. Now we have it marked."

"Well, what are we waiting for?"

Edith gave a puffy laugh, "The hooded avenger. These are pros, Oakesie. Taking them isn't going to be easy, and Chiliman is a dedicated and obsessed man. Dedicated to disposing of the entire team. He'd like nothing better than you steaming in to save the fair damsel. That's probably exactly how he sees it."

"It's how I see it as well," Boysie bridled.

Edith turned to Couperose, telling him to get every detail available on the Villa Veronique. "We'll take them," he said firmly, "but we'll do it my way."

Boysie suddenly found himself becoming romantic.

"The bugger's got Zizi there. I want him. I just don't think we should hang about."

"Scientifically," snapped Edith.

***

Couperose took an hour, but it was time well spent. He came back, not only with the exact location of the villa, but with diagrams of the place - plan and elevation. His man from Avignon was still watching and there had apparently been no sign of movement since the trio had been deposited there. Boysie became tense, wondering what they might be doing with Zizi, his overactive imagination throwing up all sorts of conjured pictures of tortures and interrogations. The romantically-sounding Villa Veronique became, in his mind, a medieval dungeon with decor by De Sade - iron maidens, racks, thumb screws, and the more painful articles of the trade, all about as subtle as a flame thrower.

The promontory of Cap Martin lies a little up the coast from the territorial boundary between France and the Principality of Monaco. It is tree-covered and dotted with villas, for it was once the most fashionable winter resort on the coast. The grand villas have now been taken over for other uses, but some of the smaller ones remain as permanent homes, or holiday hideaways.

The Villa Veronique is one of these, set on the eastern side of the spit, surrounded on three sides by a wall in which large wrought-iron gates are set back from the road.

Edith, Couperose, the two heavies and Boysie studied the plans for a long time, noting the general layout of its two storeys and small cellar, how the entrance hall led straight into a large main room, with a kitchen off to the right and high French windows which, in turn, opened out to a patio from whence steps dropped to a small jetty and bathing area.

Upstairs there were four bedrooms and a large bathroom, the master bedroom with a wide balcony overlooking the jetty. The cellar was intended for wine and gave room only for the swinging of a couple of fair-sized cats.

"Dusk would be the time to take them," Edith said. "From both sides. A party going over the wall and a couple of launches coming in from the sea. What kind of transport have they got?" he asked Couperose.

"The Peugeot isn't in sight, probably in the garage or even removed altogether. There's a black Renault, which was drawn up in front of the main door when I last spoke to my man, and there's some kind of boat at the jetty, and a couple of pedallos."

"Dusk tomorrow," Edith concluded.

"It's a hell of a time off," grumbled Boysie. "They could have Zizi carved up and dumped in the sea by then. Why not dawn?"

"They'll be alert at dawn. If they're on the qui vive."

"Qui vive, qui schmive," Boysie sounded disgusted. "There's a bird in there being maimed, driven out of her mind."

"Quell the melodrama, old lad. They're probably merely chatting her up."

"Chatting her up with scourges."

"If my fellow from Avignon hears screams, we'll precipitate matters," grinned Couperose.

Boysie remained silent while Edith and Couperose went into details concerning who would do what, and from where the reinforcements would come: apparently five people from DTS were flying in later, and Couperose was bringing some of his men up from Paris.

"Which reminds me," Boysie dragging himself from the nagging worry about Zizi. "What's happened to Griffin and Lyric?"

William Edith smiled a sick leer, "They'll be around, I've no doubt, Boysie, no doubt at all."

XV - DAWN CHORUS

A substantial flock of birds breaking into song at first light

Boysie insisted on having some personal armament more effective than the Beretta. Nobody appeared to mind very much, and Couperose produced a Colt -38 Super and three spare magazines. They then decided to meet first thing in the morning, by which time the additional bodies would have arrived.

"You don't mind if I go and get myself some gear?" Boysie asked deferentially. "Mine's got spread around a bit."

"You okay for money?" Edith seemed actually concerned.

"I'll manage. I just want another sweater and some clean drawers."

Everyone seemed to think it was a good idea, and Boysie left the hotel, turning sharp left and disappearing into the streets which surrounded the Rue de France. The shops were all open, goodies displayed and tempting. There was a time in his life when Boysie could not have resisted the suedes, leathers and silks which shrieked elegantly from the male boutiques. But now he knew better, and satisfied himself with a moderately priced cord battledress, a cheap leather belt, a black roll neck, two pairs of black socks, a pair of black sneakers and a couple of spare pairs of black briefs, without any fancy animal patterns on the front.

Walking back to the hotel he paused at an ironmonger's establishment and, almost instinctively, entered and purchased a hunting knife, with sheath. It was cheap but sharp and would be effective. On his way out he spotted some large leather pistol holders and pouches marked up as Army surplus, so he bought one of each and completed the shopping spree with a ball of thin twine.

It was only a vague plan; so vague that he could not even own to it yet, but it was there, having a lurk in the back of his head; a kind of private fantasy which he was acting out, knowing well enough that he could never bring himself to make the leap from the idea to reality.

He collected his key from the desk, went up to the room and rang room service for a plate of smoked salmon, a large vodka, a quarter bottle of brandy, and a jug of coffee.

The food arrived and for the next hour Boysie ate, drank and lazed on the bed, toying with his problem. After that he started to think again.

William Edith was wrong, he knew it in his guts, his water and his bones. If Chiliman and his crew had Zizi cooped up in the Villa Veronique and imagined she knew where Boysie would head, then tomorrow night would be far too late. Already it might be too late. He sipped black coffee, his mind crammed with images of the lush Zizi Portobello suffering agonies in the cellar which was only big enough to swing a couple of fair-sized cats.

The mental chain reaction continued, cats became sinister and Zizi's pleasing body took hold of Boysie's senses. By tomorrow night it would be out of sight. There were two choices, he told himself: go above William Edith and make a complaint at the local police station, or do something about it himself.

Boysie did not like police stations as he had this old streak of snobbery which led 1-tru to believe that you did not meet a nice class of person in police stations. As for really doing something about it himself, that, he concluded, would be dangerous and stupidly romantic.

Other images, the pictures of childhood, flooded in-a white knight on a charger thundering over rough ground towards a white castle. The knight reined in the horse, which pawed the ground with its hooves and blew thick steam from its nostrils. From a high slitted window, the princess leaned out crying, "Save me, sir knight." The knight hefted his lance and pushed back his visor.

Boysie groaned. He looked ridiculous in that white armour.

It was madness. Stupid. He swung his legs off the bed and went through to the bathroom, found a large plastic laundry bag, pushed a bath towel into it, got out his ball of twine, tied up the open end, ran the cold water until the bath was half full and immersed the plastic bag in the water. No bubbles. It was quite waterproof.

He unplugged the bath, put the bag down on the mat and went back into the bedroom to pour another cup of coffee and lie on the bed again.

After another two cups, and four more cigarettes, he began to wonder if he was fit enough. There was a time when he could swim, run, climb, jump and shoot without puffing like some wheezy bellows, or feeling his heart pounding in his head. Too many cigarettes, too much booze, not enough exercise, except with the wrong kind of women.

Zizi in the glade outside Auxerre after the sexy lunch, naked with thighs spread in obeisance and nipples reaching up in chorus to the sun, and him performing minor miracles for a man of his age and indiscretion.

"Shit," said Boysie aloud.

This time Zizi was on the scaffold, the wicked King John sat on a throne under a striped awning, together with the Sheriff of Nottingham, and the man in black (also on the scaffold) had this big glinting chopper.

An arrow whistled through the air and down went the man in black-a great cheer from the crowd-and there was Robin Hood, all in that nice Lincoln Green, cut stylishly, with some fashionable scalloping around the hem of his doublet.

The King's Men at Arms were elbowing through the crowd, but Robin galloped on towards the scaffold, reached up to swing Zizi onto the pommel of his saddle, missed and landed flat on his back.

It was all madness and, safe in that knowledge, Boysie drifted off into an uneasy sleep.

He woke suddenly and sweating. There had been a dream, though he could not recall it, except for the fact that Zizi was screaming fit to bust her bra. He looked at his watch. It was barely three o'clock and he just could not get Zizi, Chiliman, Castervermentes and Gest out of his head. It must have been Chiliman and Castervermentes he had seen outside La Mansion at Puebla in the small hours all those years ago.

Boysie got up and went back into the bathroom, undid the plastic laundry bag, took out the big towel, substituted a smaller one and began to load it with the other gear - the black cord battledress, sneakers, socks, underwear, the belt, to which he attached the holster and pouch, and, last of all, the Colt .38 Super, loaded, with the safety on and two of the spare mags in the pouch.

Then he tied the neck of the plastic sack securely and added a long loop. He put another short length of twine through the knife sheath, knotted that firmly in a loop, and carried the whole lot through to the bedroom.

He still had the little Beretta, which he checked and put into his right coat pocket. Last of all, Boysie uncorked the brandy, took a long pull, replaced the cork and stuck the bottle into his left pocket.

Then he rang down to the desk and told them he wanted to go out and take some pictures at sunrise and could they have a cab ready for him in half-an-hour. He still knew that he would not really do it, so he stretched out on the bed again, lit another cigarette and waited for the desk to call him back. In any case, he thought, they probably had orders to report his movements to William Edith and that would put an end to his foolishness.

But thirty-five minutes later the telephone rang and a bright feminine voice told him that his car was waiting. Another slug of brandy and Boysie slung the plastic sack over his shoulder and headed out of the room. The white knight and Robin Hood were both on their way to the rescue, though he knew well enough that, when he came to it, he would not do anything at all: it was far too dangerous.

The car was a Merc of some kind: black with a driver who looked like a tired llama. Boysie told him to take the corniche inferieur and drop him off on the other side of Roquebrune. Boysie knew exactly where he wanted to be left - just where the road cuts across the neck of Cap Martin.

The driver looked puzzled and Boysie pointed to the plastic laundry sack and burbled something about taking photographs. The llama driver shrugged: what did he care anyway? The Negresco was nothing more than a luxurious lunatic asylum.

It was still very dark when the car dropped him. Boysie lit a cigarette and stood in the shadows of the trees, watching the tail lights recede towards Nice, and wished he had kept the torch.

He sat down by the roadside and waited for the first break in the blackness which would herald the beginning of dawn. It took two cigarettes before he could see enough to head through the trees, over the hard red earth towards the dangerously sharp rocks at the eastern lip of the cape. The climb down was not easy, but the sea below was calm, lapping at the clustered boulders. He was out of breath by the time he got within spitting distance of the water, but it was now light, and to his left he could see the sweep of the coast and the rising houses of Carnoles and Menton. Boysie had a slight flicker of nostalgia-it seemed a long time ago since he had last been here, on a sneaked weekend with Mostyn's secretary, the lovely Iris Macintosh a lustful romp which had inevitably led to tragedy.

Boysie shook his head and turned to look at the immediate shoreline of Cap Martin, counting the villas. Veronique was about half a mile along, the fourth house, he could see it quite clearly, its dirty cream wall dropping into the sea.

The light was grey, an odd silent and unreal stillness, as though he was the only person alive on this piece of shore. Even the water made little noise. He realised that he was straining his ears for something. The dawn chorus? They don't have one here, he reflected, and two other images slid into the panovision screen of his head: an afternoon, long ago, with his one-time steady, Elizabeth, driving not far from here, high up across the Alpes Maritimes to Grasse, the air thin and everything bathed in bright sunlight and perfect stillness, no creatures moving, no sign of life; the other picture, superimposed almost, was of a misty morning of his childhood in Berkshire, standing in a wood with a girl called Ruth or Sybil or Daphne or something, and the whole sky cracking open with bird song, and he knew - it was the very pinpointed moment that he knew - it was not going to last for ever.

Slowly, Boysie took the Beretta out of his pocket, slid the magazine from the butt, pumped the action once and threw the two pieces of metal into the sea. Then he started to undress.

It was chilly and he felt a little absurd, bare-arsed on the rocks, his clothes lying in a pathetic little pile at his feet. It was only then that he knew he should have tied a loop of twine around the neck of the brandy bottle as well. He was going to need something to warm him at the other end.

Well, he thought, you can't have it both ways, uncorking the bottle and tipping quite a lot of the liquid fire down his throat. It brought tears to his eyes and made him wonder what the hell he was doing, stark stripped on a chilly dawn. Decisions, he pondered, decisions, hanging the hunting knife around his neck, and then the plastic sack of clothes. The rocks hurt his feet, and as he neared the water he was certain that he had spotted several lumps of excrement bobbing jolly on the sea.

The water was cold, the plastic sack ungainly around his neck, floating ahead of him. After the first three cautious strokes, Boysie was convinced that this was how he was at last going to lose his manhood. What a way for it to go, he mused, chilled off and frozen blue in the Med. He smiled, it had been blue before.

Steadying himself in the water, Boysie aimed for the dirty creamy wall of the Villa Veronique - which seemed a hundred miles away now - and began to swim slowly but steadily towards it.

XVI - BARCAROLLE

Song or instrumental piece suggestive of boating in swaying 6/8 time

They always say death by drowning is not an unpleasant way to go - what with the biopic flashing through your mind and all that. Boysie nearly went, but he did not find it reassuring.

His leg and arm muscles felt as though they were being wrenched out of place and near capitulation, while at one point his wind gave out altogether, making him turn over on his back and lie there floating, head thrust upwards, mouth open and wheezing, gasping for air.

But survival was important, so he pressed on, fighting the fatigue, the undertow and cold, his head bobbing in and out of the water which misted his eyes. At times, through the haze, he glimpsed the target villa, and it seemed to remain as far away as ever.

Halfway across he slewed to the right, moving inshore, instinctively searching for shallow water in case the most feared cramps would catch up with him.

Eventually, after what seemed to be a hundred years, he found himself only fifty yards or so from his goal. Then the other terror began to penetrate the numbness, making him forget the perils of cramp and the ebbing strength of his limbs.

He craned his neck back, trying to scout the villa and its surrounding area, searching for any sign of life which might bring the crack and sudden oblivion of a bullet. He recalled a hundred movies which showed graphically how a swimmer got shot: the flurry of water, the body heeling over and the spreading crimson patch.

He wanted to throw up with fear and exertion.

There were no shots, no sudden shrieks of pain or blood. Rocks washed past him, and, slightly surprised, Boysie realised that he had made it, clinging to a rusty iron ring set into the buttress of the jetty which shielded him from the rising villa above. He clung on, panting and spent, aware, once more, of the silence and terrible cold surrounding his naked body.

He hung there until his breathing returned almost to normal, and vision cleared so that he was able to look around with fresh interest. To the left, steps ran up to the jetty and villa.

Still the silence, except for the sound of a train, wafting over the water from a long way off; but he was now acutely aware that something was not quite right - a renewed wariness creeping into his head. It had something to do with the description of the villa. Something either William Edith or Couperose had said.

He let go of the ring and began to founder, lashing out in a moment of panic towards the steps. The stone was slippery from years of wear and tear, from the sloshing sea. His hand could not gain a hold at first, but finally he pulled himself up, lying across the lowest steps, half in and half of the water like a seal. They would probably be down in a minute, he reflected, to ring the bell and throw fish for him to catch.

"There's some kind of boat at the jetty, and a couple of pedallos," Couperose had said. That was the kicker, because there was no kind of boat here and not a pedallo in sight. Furthermore, as he looked up the steps, Boysie saw a legend burned out on a wooden plaque. *Villa Bougainvillea* the plaque said, and Boysie wanted to cry.

He was exhausted, cold and in the wrong place. The depression lasted about two minutes; then Boysie started to rationalise. He had swum either too far or not far enough, and there was only one thing to do now: get back in the water and find his bearings.

Boysie closed his eyes, slipped into the sea, rolling onto his back with the plastic sack floating on top of him, just below his chest, frog-pushing with his legs to propel him from the shore. To help concentration he counted each kick.

At twenty-three he stopped, floating and looking back over his toes. The right big toenail needed trimming. To the left, just above the Villa Bougainvillea, nestling among rocks and trees, was another villa. It had a balcony overlooking the sea just like in the plan Couperose had shown them, and there was a little boat tied up at the jetty, moored clear of the rocks. There was also a pair of shabby pedallos lashed near the steps. No sign of life.

Boysie took a deep breath, rolled over and began a slow tired swim towards the boat, pleased that there were no visible guards, and thinking that it was bloody early in the morning which was as good a reason as any for there being nobody around.

As he came closer to the jetty he realised that the steps up to the villa were not the only means of access. The wooded area, which was a kind of garden, to the right of the house, sloped gently down to a tiny shingle beach, a pocket among the rocks: a place which afforded plenty of cover from the building.

He had reached the boat now, an eleven-foot Dore Sports, one hand touching the hull. Treading water, Boysie began to feel around for the hunting knife, realising that he would have to be very careful. If it slipped, point down into the water, it could cause him a nasty mischief: the unkindest cut of all.

The Dore Sports was tied up to a ring in the jetty wall with a big spreading and sprawling knot. Not a very nautical knot. He got the knife out and began to saw at the rope. It took about four hacks before parting. He trod water again, like running hard against an escalator, manoeuvring the knife back into its sheath. By the time he had completed the operation the little boat had begun to sway away, floating a good six feet from the wall.

Boysie trundled round it, pushing lightly. It wallowed off, slowly but with its mind obviously made up.

He paid no attention to the pedallos. They were not the fastest craft known to those who go down to the sea in ships. In any case, if he got away with it, Boysie had no intention of leaving that way.

He clambered round the rocks and up onto the little shingle beach, the stones biting into his feet, taking just two staggering steps before his thighs gave out and he buckled to the ground, neatly avoiding a small pile deposited by some passing dog.

Let them come down here and shoot me, he thought. He was quite exhausted and would probably die there anyway. The idea of being shot galvanised him into action again, and he got the knife out fast.

The twine around the neck of the sack parted easily and he routed around, getting the Colt out first, flicking off the safety and placing it among the stones where he could grab it fast. Then he hauled out the towel, rubbing his body to get the circulation going again as much as to dry himself. He felt incredibly vulnerable and could not really see himself going into action, with the automatic pistol, dressed as a streaker.

As life began to return, Boysie climbed wearily to his feet, lost his balance and stepped right into the dog shit.

He swore and staggered down to the water's edge, keeping low, to wash the soiled foot, then back again, half crouching, pulling on his clothes, pushing his feet into the sneakers and buckling on the belt, to which he had now added the knife sheath.

The exhaustion seemed to be passing, though his thighs and calves trembled with a will of their own when he stood up, the Colt ready in his right hand.

Stupidly he wished that he had a mirror. He had always fancied himself in black. At least nobody would mistake him for a vacuum cleaner salesman in this gear. He only needed the wide-brimmed hat and he could have played the Jack Palance part in *Shane*. Then he remembered that Jack Palance got dead in *Shane* so he went back to Central Casting for another role.

Standing there on the beach, hidden from the house by the rocks and trees, Boysie considered that he had already proved William Edith wrong on one count. It was well past dawn and nobody was alert at the Villa Veronique.

His stomach did an impressive imitation of someone plunging from a tall building. What if it was already over and finished, with Zizi gone, or dead? There was only one way to find out, and that called for more decisions. If you are alone you cannot rush a house, that is a law of nature and survival: you just do not do it if you want to stay alive. In this kind of situation there is one of two choices: either you go to the front door, rouse everyone, do a number on the melon of the fellow who opens up, and take your chances with the rest; or you do it by stealth and shrewd cunning-which means that you hang about, wait and let the inhabitants make the first move, then deal with them according to circumstances. That was the best way.

Boysie hung about.

For two hours he hung about, crouched off the beach, close to the villa wall, expecting someone to look out from the balcony, notice that the boat had got sea fever, and start getting angry.

Two hours was a long time to wait, particularly without the natural comforts of life, like a drink, or smoke, or a jelly baby on which to nibble.

It was getting on for nine o'clock before the first signs of life were made apparent. There was the sound of a lock being activated at the front of the house, and a door opening.

Boysie shuffled along the wall and peered out from the shelter of a clump of bushes. He recognised the man who was unlocking the door of the black Renault parked in the small drive. Couperose had shown him the mug-shot: Frelon - the Hornet.

Frelon yawned, trudged the few yards up to the gates, which he unlocked and pulled open. He then walked back, got behind the wheel of the car, started the engine, raced it like he was on the grid at Brand's, and took off as though Dracula was after him in a jet hearse.

Boysie did some rapid calculations. With Frelon gone the villa should contain Zizi, plus Chiliman, Castervermentes and Gest: though there was possibly one other, because Couperose had said the trio had been met at Cap Martin station and nobody would have left Zizi alone in the villa. He was pondering this possibility when the shout of rage came from the rear of the house. Someone had noticed that the Dore Sports had got away.

There was a lot of banging and clattering. The front door of the house opened again and a short man, dressed in jeans and a faded blue shirt came running out, obviously trying to stop Frelon. But he was long gone and the man in blue threw up his arms in a melodramatic gesture, letting fly to the morning air with a gabble of his native tongue and much repetition of the word merde. He then got careless and went back into the house without shutting the door.

There appeared to be a conference going on at the rear: a lot of talking, some shouting - one very angry voice raised above the others - and a lot of language which would have offended most God-fearing people. In fact it was like an ordinary family party when relatives have not seen one another for a long time.

Boysie decided that the moment had come and, breaking cover, he walked round to the front of the house, heading for the open main door. He was only half-a-dozen steps away when the little man in the blue shirt came barrelling out and it was difficult to determine which of them was the most surprised.

The little man skidded to a halt, his mouth open. Boysie just stood there and let time pass. Then the one in the blue shirt seemed to recover himself and half turned, the muscles around his mouth beginning to operate properly, head going back to yell a warning. The head was still back when Boysie hit him with the heel of his pistol butt just behind the left ear.

Boysie grinned, realising that was what had been missing in his life for the last hours. All the pent up frustration and anger needed to come out in some concrete manner like hitting somebody hard. The end product was a short Frenchman in jeans and a blue shirt lying in a heap on the gravel. Boysie grinned again - the heap would have a nasty lump and a headache when he woke up. Serve the bugger right, he thought, picking his way over the fallen lump heading towards the door.

From the hallway he could see the entire ensemble out on the patio behind the big French windows at the rear of the main room: there was a short grossly fat and oily man whom he took to be Chiliman, a younger, more agile and slim man whom he positively recognised as the singer, Gest, and the third could only be Castervermentes, swarthy with olive skin - he kept raising his arms in a flapping motion, letting the hands drop back onto his thighs, a gesture of frustration as he looked out to sea.

"You could get it with one of the pedallos," he kept saying. "James is fit enough, but with my weak ankle I dare not go."

"And what about my chest and heart?" Chiliman made a lot of noise when he shouted: with any luck, Boysie thought, he will have a heart attack on the spot.

"All right, all right," Castervermentes shrugged. "It's no good waiting for Henri to get back. James and Edgar can catch it." He was leering at Gest, "You've got good thigh muscles, haven't you, James?"

Gest said something quiet which did not sound nice, then Chiliman started to shout for Edgar who could not hear him on account of the fact that he was unconscious and lying with a mouthful of gravel in front of the house.

It was at this moment that Boysie noticed the door by the stairs. The door had been shown on the plan, and it led to the cellar. There was a large key in the lock.

Zizi was his first consideration and he was at the door in a second, turning the key, opening it and entering, taking the key with him and locking the door on the inside.

There was a light just inside the door, which was as well because the stone steps were steep and narrow. Boysie scuttled down them aware of the chill which surrounded him. The steps led off into the narrow cellar, one side of which was given up to stone bottle racks. There were no bottles, but at the far end, huddled and wrapped in blankets, on a small camp bed, lay Zizi Portobello, her face turned towards him in fear and apprehension. There were bruises down one side of her face, the right eye was swollen and blackened and her lips were puffed and caked with blood.

"Boyzee," the voice trailed off, low.

"Who did that?" Boysie lifted her in his arms, the blankets falling away to reveal that she was only clad in panties and bra.

Zizi began to cry, and through the tears, she whispered, "I'm okay, Boyzee. But zey 'ave you now."

"No, they 'aven't me," said Boysie, feeling the fury rise. "They don't even know I'm here."

There was shouting and noise from above.

"Wrong," he said. "They know someone's here now. Who did it?"

"Zee dark one, zee one zey call Casterversomething."

"Castervermentes. I'll kill that bastard."

"Zee fat one, 'ee stood by and tell 'im to do eet. I'm okay though, Boyzee, look, I can stand, not like zee other one."

"What other one?"

"Zee other girl. Zee one zey 'ave killed and put in zee sea. Zee one called Lyric."

"They killed Lyric?"

"She ees dead. Zey tell me that and tell me zey will do zee same to me."

"Judas Iscariot on a tandem." Boysie felt his wrath exploding, far down in his guts and then, like a fire, in his head. He knew now what they meant when they talked about people seeing red. "Stay there," he hissed. "It'll be okay now, Zizi."

He went back up the steps, two at a time, pressing his ear to the door at the top. It was as cold as a snowman's armpit, even up there at the top of the cellar steps, but the sounds from outside, in the main house, seemed a long way off.

Boysie turned the key gently and peeped out. Nobody, only the voices coming from the front of the house where they were obviously trying to bring the world back to the somnolent Edgar.

“Someone hit him,” he heard Castervermentes say.

Then, “The boat, it’ll be far gone. We’ve got to do something about the boat. You get to it and I’ll look after Edgar.”

“I can’t ...” Chiliman started.

“All right, so we lose the boat.”

Then a muttering and some French and the sound of someone retching. Edgar was coming back to life.

Boysie realised that he could not stand there, out in the open, all day. He gently closed the cellar door behind him, locked it from the outside, slipped the key into his battledress pocket, and padded through to the main living room. Behind him he could hear them helping Edgar back into the house.

The kitchen door was on his right, a swing door. Boysie swung through it and waited. It took about two minutes to bring Edgar into the main room. Then they obviously sat him down and started to argue about the boat, which had, it seemed, drifted out into the middle of the bay and then hit the doldrums.

“It could start drifting again any time now,” Castervermentes said. “And we’re going to need it later. Edgar’s not fit enough, look at him. You’ll have to try.”

Gest laughed, “Come on, Caesar. We’ll have a go. Exercise will do you good.”

Chiliman just appeared to be wheezing and there was a moaning noise which, presumably, came from the luckless Edgar. Then the sounds moved in the direction of the patio. He could hear noises which suggested that they were going down the steps to the jetty.

Boysie pushed against the door as though it was wired for an explosion. Edgar sat in a leather chair, his head in his hands and his back towards Boysie.

Boysie hit him again, on the left side this time. Poor Edgar would probably end up with scrambled brains. In the meantime, he ended up on the floor, making a lot of noise about it.

They heard that down on the jetty and someone came running up the steps. Boysie stood in the centre of the open French windows, holding the Colt with both hands, square on to the rising target.

It was Castervermentes.

"Stay," said Boysie quietly. "Stay and tell your friends to come up, and you can get your hands over your head before I give you some sudden terminal brain damage."

He should have seen the flicker in Castervermentes' eyes. The mouth broke into a slow smile and he took another pace forward up the steps.

Just before the flash and wave of pain; just before the ground came up to meet him; just before darkness descended, Boysie realised that Harry the Hornet must have got back.

***

When he began to take interest again, Boysie swore internally. He had come within an ace of getting it together, but Castervermentes and Chiliman had a full house, a very full house once Frelon had crept quietly back.

His head felt like it had been amputated, and even Zizi's hand, cool on his forehead, could not stop the pneumatic drills which were being operated by Wimpey gangers inside his skull.

He tried to sit up, but the moment he raised his head the people from Wimpey got cracking with a miniature steam shovel.

" 'Eet's okay, Boyzee," crooned Zizi. She looked terrible, with the bruises and swellings.

"Bastards," murmured Boysie. "Sorry."

"You were most brave," she said, and he thought he could detect tears in her eyes, which was not surprising because when you get thumped in the eyes you tend to leak from the lachrymal passages.

"Whasatime?" He managed to prop himself on one elbow, gritting his teeth against the pain.

Zizi took hold of his hand and squinted down at his watch.

"Your clock says twelve," she tried to smile.

The memories came back in a rush. No wonder he felt half dead: the swim and his one man act of vengeance. This place looked uncompromisingly secure. If they were going to get out they would need some of Houdini's magic. Depression. Boysie thought, mentally banging his head against the stone to find a way out. But his thought processes seemed to be clogged. There was no obvious way. The cellar was desperately cold which meant his senses were getting back to normal. With the cold he remembered Lyric and what Zizi had said.

"I wonder why they didn't finish me off," he mumbled. "Like Lyric. Tell me about Lyric."

"I only know what I 'eard, Boyzee. Last night zee one called Edgar was talking to Henri - 'ee was zee one who ..."

"Who got hold of you at Chalon."

"Yes. I 'eard them talking last night and Edgar said something about the girl's body in the car. Henri said it was a pity about 'er, but Edgar said she knew too much. I only know zey talked about the girl Lyric because zey were saying zat 'er name was pretty."

"You said she sounded like cheap soap."

Through the bruises and swellings, Zizi looked sad, "Did you," she began, "did you care for 'er?"

"I hardly knew her. I met her brother once. He's dead as well, now." Privately he wondered what had happened to Griffin. "They put her in the sea, you said."

"When zey talked zey said later zey would put 'er corpse in the sea."

Boysie did not have to think much further than that. He had screwed it and implicated Zizi. They would undoubtedly end up with Lyric, very dead and very wet. Sea food. The refrain of an old scatty pop song of his youth came seeping into his head, unwanted -

Hold tight, hold tight,
Hold tight, hold tight,
Foodly-yacky-zacky,
Want some sea food,
Mama.
Shrimps and rice,
They're very nice.

He was the last on Chiliman's list and, presumably, they were only keeping him alive until the last moment in case they had to barter. He thought again and realised this was unlikely also. Chiliman had been utterly ruthless and there was no reason to believe that he would be anything else now. The one slim hope lay in nasty little William Edith and his merry men, but they would not make a move until dusk: and dusk was a long time away.

They lay there for the best part of an hour. Cold, wretched and with Boysie wishing someone had an aspirin.

At last there was the sound of a key turning in the lock, up the steps.

Castervermentes came down with the man Boysie recognised as Henri Frelon.

"Don't get up," said Castervermentes flashing his gold teeth. He was flashing the Colt which Boysie had intended to use on him.

"Do it now," said Boysie wearily.

"Not quite yet. We will soon be going and it will be done before we leave. There is one piece of information we would like."

"Name, rank and serial number," said Boysie. He had heard them do that in old movies on television. It sounded right.

"Your friends at the Negresco," Castervermentes continued undeterred. "We would like to know if they plan anything, or if you were their one man army."

"Screw you."

Castervermentes shrugged. "It doesn't matter. We could have done a deal."

"Not interested in deals," Boysie heard himself say, puzzled that he could say anything so stupid.

Castervermentes laughed aloud: a stagey kind of laugh suitable for baddies in B movies. "Not a deal for you, only for the girl. You were dead anyway, Oakes. We had our man in Nice. He would have hit you by now in any case, so you're already living on borrowed time. The girl you could have saved."

Boysie glanced at Zizi, desperate to play for more time. "All right," he said, making it sound sullen, "All right. I don't know if they'll try anything else. They were going to leave it alone anyway. Coming was my own idea, for the sake of the girl. There's nobody backing me up and I'm not very important to them now, so I don't suppose ..."

"They've got fresh reinforcements," chuckled Castervermentes. "I'll give you the benefit of the doubt though. Perhaps you don't know what they intend. Nobody but an idiot would have tried it alone." He started to back away.

"You have about one hour. Make the most of it."

He had difficulty getting up the steps backwards. Frelon went up the proper way. The door closed again and the key turned in the lock.

When Boysie looked down, Zizi was crying.

There had to be some way. Gingerly he got to his feet. His thighs and arm muscles were stiff as rusty hinges and the gang from Wimpey in his head had been replaced by some demented dwarfs with buzz saws. They were working on all the most sensitive nerves. He retched; swallowed; squeezed his eyes shut and then open again, reaching out with his hand for support against the stone wine rack. The stones moved against his hand. Fresh interest sparked and then kindled.

Boysie began to examine the wine rack. It was not a permanent structure, but an assembly of tiles laid over bricks. He reached up to the topmost tile and pulled. It came away easily, and he stood there, weighing it in his hand, his eyes moving between the bricks and tiles and the stone steps which led up to the door.

It was very risky, but what the hell, you only die one time. As he thought it, Boysie knew that was not true either. In the years since he had known the late lamented James George Mostyn, he had died a thousand times.

If he was going to stop it happening for real, he would have to be quick. There was a lot of work to be done and less than an hour in which to do it.

XVII - SHANTY

The work had to be done quickly, with as little noise as possible. Considering the exertions, his sapped strength, the egg on his head and the binding of his muscles, Boysie got organised with remarkable speed.

Zizi assisted, not helped by the chill of the cellar, clad only in her underwear. It was also not conducive for work, as far as Boysie was concerned. In the end, he made her wrap one of the blankets around herself, tucking it tightly in just below the breasts. Boysie did the tucking, an exercise which proved to him once more that there was plenty of life still in him. It helped motivate the determination to survive.

He first began dismantling part of the wine rack, dodging quietly up the steps, gradually building a loose pile of bricks and slates on the third step from the top: an unsteady and badly balanced pile which came level with the top of the step and leaned precariously outwards. Anyone putting a foot heavily on top of the pile would crash and slide forward with little chance of regaining balance in the narrow flight.

Once the obstacle was completed, Boysie untied his right sneaker, took off his sock and pulled it over his right hand. Standing on tiptoe and leaning forward on the step immediately below the hazard, he could just reach the electric bulb which lighted the steps. With the sock protecting his hand, Boysie removed the bulb.

While the bottom steps were still illuminated by the small light in the cellar ceiling, the top steps were now in total darkness. True there would be some light from the open door, but that was a risk which had to be taken.

Getting his sock and sneaker back on again, Boysie continued to dismantle the rack, this time using only the heavy bricks, building up a dry wall, two bricks thick at an angle where the steep stone steps ended and the rack itself began. The wall jutted out to the length of roughly four to five feet and, within half an hour, it had risen to a height of about three feet, giving a V-shaped sheltered area in which Zizi could crouch with comfort, her body shielded from any flying fragments of metal-like bullets.

There was also just room for Boysie to squat down behind her and at least have the front of his body protected.

With luck he reckoned the wall would not be necessary, but the work kept them warm and occupied. Throughout he glanced constantly at his wrist, watching the hands move steadily towards one. At five past they heard the key in the lock.

"Down." Boysie had already instructed her, and Zizi crushed herself into the shelter as if she was trying to burrow through the cellar wall. Boysie pressed close in on her back, his body turned to the left, his big right paw curled around one of the bricks.

There was an irritated noise from the doorway above, and Castervermentes said something about the bloody light bulb going. Then movement.

Castervermentes hit the brick and tile obstacle with his full weight. He gave a snort and a short yelp of surprise, then, as his foot slipped, he lost balance and came hurtling down the steps.

Boysie vaguely heard the yell from above as he leaped forward onto the moving body as it landed, sprawling, at the foot of the steps. His hand went up, clutching the brick, then descended hard and fast, knocking the wind and consciousness out of the flailing Castervermentes.

As before, he had been carrying the Colt. Boysie's hand snaked out to wrench it from his grasp almost before the brick had done its work.

Turning on the balls of his feet, acting totally on instinct, Boysie fired twice up the stairs: once from the hip as his hand moved up, then one aimed shot at the figure silhouetted in mid-spin in the doorway.

The second bullet was not necessary. Frelon was already dying when it hit him, its only useful purpose being to stop the twisting body and send it flying away from the door.

He was already halfway up the steps when Frelon hit the ground. Twice Boysie almost slipped on the rubble which was now strewn right down to the cellar floor. At the top step he paused, shouting back to Zizi. "Thump him with another brick if he wakes up."

Then he leaped into the hallway.

Sore-headed Edgar was stumbling out of the main room with a revolver in his hand, his face masked in panic. Boysie did not have time to think. As far as he was concerned this was the practice range at the Department's training centre. Anything that moved got blasted. Edgar got blasted, his face assuming a look of incredulity as he arched backwards in a graceful motion as though performing some clever dive from the top board.

Behind the lifting body, Boysie glimpsed Chiliman and Gest, out on the patio, turned towards him, their faces white masks, frozen with the sudden event. For a second, the world seemed to petrify Edgar's body in mid-air; Boysie, still with the shock waves tingling his arm; and the two others stone in the sunlight outside: a still life of violence.

Then Gest moved, lunging to his left, an arm reaching out for something beyond Boysie's vision.

Boysie adjusted into a forward firing stance, legs apart and both hands on the weapon.

"I'm going to mince both of you," he yelled, his mouth dry. "They're for starters, this is the main course."

As he shouted he realised Gest had got what he wanted and was rolling away to his left. For a second Boysie was indecisive, not knowing which target to choose.

Then the shots ripped from Gest's gun and Boysie had to drop flat, three, then four, bullets shattering into the hall, flaying plaster from the walls.

Behind him something smashed. It sounded like a mirror. Seven years' bad luck for Gest. There was the whine of a ricochet in the confined space and Boysie was well down, belly to the red tiles, snaking his way backwards towards the cellar door, firing twice without looking or aiming.

He reached the steps and fired again. Two more shots answered him. Then another, tearing a chunk of wood from the jamb. Then silence.

Panting, smelling the fear on him, Boysie lay just within the cellar steps. It took him a good two minutes to get his breath back and realise what was going on out on the sea side of the house. All the time Zizi was shouting from below in the cellar, shrieking to him and asking if he was all right.

Slowly he rose to his feet and carefully looked out. No shots. He moved, crouching, forward into the living room. On the table he saw his spare magazines and grabbed one of them before moving out onto the patio.

Below, on the smooth unruffled sea, Chiliman and Gest were bobbing in one of the pedallos, both pedalling hard and away from the jetty. Boysie smiled, knowing that at least they had not got the boat, then Chiliman turned and his hand came up and the bullets started to crack again.

Boysie dropped, crawled back, raced into the house and up the stairs.

He was almost at the top, his mind focused on the main bedroom with its balcony which would give him a wide arc of fire into the sea, when he heard the cry from the cellar, and the sound of scuffling and feet on the steps.

Castervermentes was coming through the cellar door with Zizi in front of him, her arm locked hard behind her back, lips moving but no sound.

"I'm getting to the car," Castervermentes' face was parchment grey and there was blood soaking down onto the shoulder of his white jacket. He began to back away, keeping Zizi between them, the woman's face twisted with fear.

There was a trick to this situation and Boysie had only the one chance. Castervermentes would be weak and groggy, even on the verge of panic. Boysie lifted the automatic and prayed there would be no ricochets.

He fired twice, wide but close enough to make Castervermentes believe he was prepared to go the whole way. The Latin American let out a grunt and threw Zizi towards Boysie, as though thrusting her at the next shot, turning and starting to run for the main door.

"Down Zizi," he shrieked and, as she hit the tiles, he saw the blur of Castervermentes' head and shoulders in his sights. He squeezed twice and gasped as the target's head began to fragment in a horrible blossom of bone and gore, the red mist seeming to hang motionless in the doorway as the body swallowed out towards the gravel.

Zizi gave a sobbing little cry and Boysie, arm limp now as though weighed down by the gun, leaned over the banister and retched.

He wiped the back of his mouth and tumbled down the stairs to Zizi who lay in a little heap, sobbing.

"I'm not going to let the others get away." His breathing was bad so that he gasped the words out, fighting his pumping lungs. "You all right?"

Zizi nodded, her lips clamped together.

"I need your help," he was slipping the empty magazine out of the Colt, slapping the new one in place. "You any strength left?"

She nodded again, still tight-lipped, and Boysie grabbed her hand, half pulling and dragging her through the living room and out to the patio.

Gest and Chiliman were still pedalling, their little craft moving steadily away towards the tip of the cape. The remaining pedallo bobbed against the jetty.

"Come on."

Zizi took a step forward, realised she was hampered by the blanket and pulled it off. They ran down the steps and Boysie untied the pedallo, holding it for Zizi as she clambered in, before he leaped into the hard slatted seat behind the wheel. The pedallo bucked with the weight, then steadied on its floats.

"You been in one of these before?"

She nodded, "Eet's very 'ard work, Boyzee, eet, 'ow you say, 'eet knockers you."

"Knackers," Boysie corrected, starting to pedal. "Too right, sweetheart; it creases you. Pedal."

He knew what the treadmill must have been like. For the first few minutes they appeared to make no headway as he strained and spun the wheel, setting their course behind the distant Chiliman and Gest who were now disappearing round the headland.

Then, as they found a rhythm, the pedallo began to move, wallowing a little at first, then picking up speed. His thigh muscles seemed to have gone through some barrier and, while they still ached, Boysie was aware that strength was returning. At least, he considered, this would get rid of the weight problem.

Zizi did not speak. He glanced at her a couple of times and saw the concentration on her face. But they kept the rhythm and, after what seemed an age, rounded Cap Martin.

The rocks along the coast, he thought, always had a brutal beauty, the grey and red, and the hard dry earth with the now faded sun-cracked buildings. It was a coast of another age, a different time when you were rich on a few thousand a year and the Blue Train had that same magic as the Orient Express, and the food was real, not plastic-packed and lifted from a freezer.

Yet the sun still sent refracted sparkles from the same sea which had been ploughed by hundreds of yachts owned by the far dead celebrities whose champagne, extravagance and dovetailed affairs still seemed to whisper spectrally when the Mistral carved down the Rhone valley and set you on edge.

Chiliman and Gest had tired fast, as though once they were out of sight from the villa they had thought themselves safe. Boysie was amazed to find that only a hundred yards or so now separated them.

"Keep going hard," he panted, lifting the Colt from the waterlogged bottom of the craft, keeping one hand on the wheel and steadying the other to get the first shot.

Neither Gest nor Chiliman looked back. They were plodding, pumping slowly through the water like a couple out on a joy ride, turning their pedallo inshore towards the beach.

Boysie knew he would be lucky to get more than a couple of shots. The way they were turning it would not be safe, for the target would soon be backed by the beach which, while not crowded in the spring sunshine, at least contained a fair sprinkling of people, including children playing at the water's edge.

As the two pedallos began the sweeping turn Boysie squeezed the trigger three times. At the first shot, Zizi's pedalling became erratic and the craft dipped. He saw the tiny plunging spray in the water to the right of Chiliman's pedallo. He did not see where the second and third shots went. They did not do any damage. He was trying to pedal and aim for another burst, realising that the angles were getting very dangerous, the point of aim becoming more and more in line with the beach, when the crack and thump of Gest's pistol made him duck.

Gest was swivelled round in the pedallo, obviously intent on emptying his weapon. But only three shots came. The first had passed harmlessly overhead, the other two were more accurate. There was a ripping, metallic clanging noise, low down on the front of the pedallo.

"Keep going," encouraged Boysie, for Zizi's strokes were getting less and less effective.

"I am out of breathing," she panted back. "Will zey kill us?"

"Not a chance," Boysie made himself laugh. "They've run out of caps."

"Caps?"

"English-type joke," he gasped, hoping he was right.

They were certainly putting every ounce of strength into their race for the beach, shouting and gesticulating - pointing back towards Boysie and Zizi - to the people on the beach.

"They're putting us in it," Boysie puffed.

"Een it?"

"In the merde, sweetie. They're dropping us in the old horse feathers; they're telling the people on the beach that we're the baddies. They'll go berserk when we hit the Mingles." He looked across at her, "And you in your ... well," he grinned, "you look jolly pretty."

"You 'ave seen me like this before, Boyzee," panting.

"I know, must be my age." Then, before he had time to swallow the words he was saying, "Zizi, love, I know it's old fashioned, but if we get out of this, will you marry me?"

They stopped pedalling, Zizi looking at him, face blank except for the contusion and cut lips, her mouth hanging open.

"You are joking?"

"No, I'm not bloody joking. It's time I settled down."

Zizi laughed, "Boyzee, you are so shellfish?"

"Real crabby."

"You mean eet? You mean will I make the nuptuals and we, what you say, we fabriquons, we manufacture, zee babies?"

"The full moment. If we get out of it. Yow ..." The pedallo was lurching violently and there were ominous glugging noises coming from the nearside float. "Jesus, we're sinking."

"Oh, Boyzee, what can I do?"

"You can't swim?"

"I can swim, but my ... what I am wearing, zey will be seen through ..."

The last two bullets must have ripped through the float which was filling with water, keeling the pedallo hard over. Ahead, Boysie saw Gest and Chiliman, sloshing through the surf, still shouting and pointing back. Some of the people on the beach were running as well. Scared of the mad rapists, Boysie thought. Boysie Oakes and Zizi Portobello Inc. Zizi and Boysie Oakes? He smiled, knowing that it was one of those ear to ear smiles which lit up his eyes.

"We're going to get wet," he chuckled. "Sink or swim together?"

“Oh, Boyzee, zis iz so sudden. We ‘ave already, well, we ‘aven’t been innocents. You must know zee screwing has for me been, well, a sort of ‘obby.”

The pedallo was really keeling over badly now, pushing them together.

“You can’t ride ‘obby ‘orses for ever. I’m in the same boat. Anyway, it isn’t just that, it’s time you settled down as well.”

The pedallo settled down, beginning its final moments.

“Dive, dive, dive,” muttered Boysie, for a second allowing his fantasies full rein-Commander Boysie von Oakes, Iron Cross with Oak Leaves, Captain of U408, the Basset hound of the Atlantic. The sea claimed his trousers and they scrambled out together, struggling shorewards. From the beach came an ominous sound, the hee-hawing noise of police arriving in large quantities.

“Should have gone down with me ship,” spluttered Boysie.

Zizi took a mouthful of water on board, lifted her head and shouted to him, “Yes. Yes, Boyzee. Yes, I will. It is romantic, no?”

XVIII - CADENCE

A progression of chords giving the effect of closing a sentence in music

When they scrambled onto the beach at last there were four gendarmes waiting for them, one holding back a knot of rubbernecks who were muttering, "*Rhubarbe-rhubarbe-rhubarbe.*"

One of the gendarmes had his pistol out and was pointing it at them. As Boysie helped Zizi up out of the surf, a couple of lads in the crowd made nudge-nudge-wink-wink noises and one of the coppers came over and wrapped his cape around her.

The gendarme with the pistol made agitated French sounds which, in turn, made Boysie angry.

"Look," he exploded, "I know you're a flick, but you've been conned, you should have nabbed the other two. I'm tired, I've been shot at, screwed up, and I've saved the princess here from a fate worse than rape. If you want to know what it's all about, you'll have to get hold of Couperose, he's at the bleeding Negresco in Nice, and take your filthy paws off me, I'm a British Intelligence officer." He reflected for a moment on the last statement. It was pretty ludicrous.

"Pardon?" grunted the French law.

"You heard," snapped Boysie, and stalked off up the beach with Zizi on his arm chattering away, explaining matters nineteen to the dozen. "Can't think why the blighters don't learn a proper language like English," he chuntered.

Needless to say, there was no sign of Chiliman or Gest.

The gendarmes took them off to the small police station at Roquebrune where several telephone calls were made, and somebody brought a skirt and blouse for Zizi.

Eventually they were shown into a small drab office which housed a melancholy Inspector who spoke moderate English.

"Your superior appears to be disenchanted with you, Monsieur Oakes."

Somewhere along his family tree the Inspector had acquired ancestors not unrelated to the bloodhound, the heavy folds of skin around his mouth and cheeks giving him a perpetually sorrowful look.

"Ah," said Boysie, clutching at Zizi's hand.

"In fact," continued the Inspector, "he asked me if there was any chance of us bringing charges against you which would ensure a life sentence in the Bastille."

"I'm not surprised."

The Inspector tried to smile through the fleshy folds. "You are to await his arrival here. He asked me to say that he will be descending upon you like the four apocalyptic horsemen."

Boysie nodded. He had known since their first meeting that he would never really see eye to eye with William Edith. Couperose and Edith, he thought, would be better off combing the area for Gest and Chiliman.

***

Gest looked at Caesar Chiliman and thought that here was a man not long for this world. The events at the Villa Veronique had wrought havoc, and their undignified escape had undoubtedly brought the fat slug near to a stroke.

Chiliman lay on the bed while Gest sat near the telephone. Since they had booked into the small pension on the outskirts of Nice, he had made one telephone call but had failed to raise the man who was contracted to hit Oakes.

Gest was surprised at his own sense of calm, for he knew that this was probably the end of the nightmare. For years, as he was trying to climb the ladder of success, he had mingled with the ruthless and cold-blooded elements of the criminal world, for they were the people who controlled the clubs and dives in which he could display the modest talent he knew was his.

That, he supposed, was why he had been such an easy mark for Castervermentes and Chiliman. Castervermentes had his own contacts, but with Gest they had constructed a modest little empire. After all, Castervermentes arranged the bookings and Gest's position as an entertainer afforded good cover enabling them to flit from city to city, setting up the contact work of death well in advance.

Chiliman had said many times that, once they completed this series of immolations, they would have a reputation in the international criminal market which could set them up for life: a kind of worldwide murder incorporated divorced from organised political or criminal groups, a fact which would make their services extremely attractive to many people.

A gangster wished some rival out of the way, or a political faction required some public figure dead, then all Castervermentes had to do was book Gest into a club in the right geographical location and the set-up could be easily organised.

But Gest was sick of it. He wished Chiliman would die, there and then, on the bed of this cheap hotel room.

The telephone buzzed and it was the man in Nice. Gest spoke to him for a few moments and then passed the instrument over to the wheezing Chiliman.

Chiliman listened for a short time and then asked, "You think it can be done then? ... Good ... Good." He paused, listening to the voice at the other end of the line. Then, "Yes, I think it best if we go out that way, it will be fast and safer, they will not expect us at the airport. Good ... We will see you then."

He replaced the telephone and smiled wearily at Gest. 177

"He assures me that it will be done and we will then go as planned."

"Into Italy?" asked Gest.

"If you are still capable of flying."

"I'm capable, but what do we do after that?"

"You leave it to me," Chiliman took a deep breath.

"I am far from finished, James. You underestimate me."

***

"You sociopathic corybanatic loon, Oakes. Mostyn warned me about you. Many times he warned me, but I did not think that even you would sink to such dangerous, disruptive and cretinous depths."

William Edith appeared to be out of sorts.

"You were wrong, you know," said Boysie, maintaining bland indifference to the verbal assault.

"Wrong, by great Kama Sutra, how wrong, Oakes?"

"Tonight would've been too late for a start. The birds would have flown, and Zizi would have been faded."

"They've flown anyway."

"Two of them, but they'll turn up. They weren't alert and waiting for us at dawn, like you said they would be."

“That’s beside the point, you moron. I was setting up an operation. You had to go and do it all by yourself, leaving a trail of carnage that’s going to take a lot of explaining.”

“You think we wouldn’t have left a trail of carnage anyway.”

“We? That’s it. We, not you, Oakes. What in hell do you think you are, a knight-errant?”

“Something like that. Zizi and I are going to be married.”

“God help me,” William Edith’s knuckles were white as he clenched his fists in rage. “Well, you’ll be the subject of a hundred enquiries before you’re finished. Married? Yes, you’ll be married all right, lad, married to a work party on the Moor. Shackled to a ball.”

“Durance vile,” Boysie said calmly. William Edith might well be a nasty little man, but his bark would be worse than his bite.

“Your honeymoon,” continued Edith, “will be spent at Her Majesty’s expense, and when she’s finished with you, I should think the authorities of this country will want you. They’ll reopen Devil’s Island for you. Seven star treatment.”

Zizi listened, fascinated and not a little blanched. There was much coming and going among both Couperose’s men and those whom Edith had summoned from London. Telephones rang and the suite at the Negresco took on the atmosphere of an operations room.

Boysie and Zizi were left alone for much of the time, after Edith had completed his verbal lashing, but the little man returned to the attack around four-thirty.

“Get your gear then,” he said in his usual soft tones which had now acquired an overlay of military authority. “There are people in London who require your presence.”

“People?” Boysie smiled, “What kind of people?”

“People in Whitehall. People who feel that you should never be allowed out on your own again. Important people.”

“People from Political Intelligence?” Boysie hazarded.

Edith gave a superior smirk, “And others. They’ve sent a lovely little Royal Air Force jet for us. It’s sitting down at the airport with the crew at the ready.”

Boysie’s stomach whipped into a frenzy. He had not expected to be reaching for the skies that quickly.

“Can Zizi come?”

"Mlle. Portobello is requested to come. She can refuse, but if she does, some of Couperose's nasties will almost certainly bring her."

"I weesh to come," Zizi stood up straight, her eyes misting like Greer Garson in Mrs. Miniver, jaw set as she had seen them do in a hundred French Resistance movies. "Nothing would keep me from Boyzee's side now. 'Ee needs me, only ..."

"Don't overdo it," Boysie hissed. "We will both come with you under protest," he looked Edith straight in his little gimlet eyes. "I have served my country well, and I have nothing to fear."

"Cut the crap, Oakes, and get yourself ready, there's a car waiting outside."

They drove out to the airport, Boysie, Edith and Zizi crammed into the back seat of a Merc, one of Couperose's men driving and an Edith heavy acting as bodyguard.

A few moments before the Merc arrived at Nice Airport, an expected VIP passenger was taken through the lounge reserved for important travellers. His clearance had been arranged earlier in the afternoon and formalities were cut to the minimum. He was an elderly, sick industrialist called Grotte, crippled and confined, for most of the time, to a wheelchair. On this occasion his personal pilot, a tall slim young man with a drooping moustache and thick dark glasses, pushed Grotte through the lounge.

Grotte was short, fat and slug-like. His aircraft, a little PA-11 Cub Special, was drawn up on the apron to the right of the main terminal, near to the line of World War One aircraft which were already warming up their engines prior to their second air circus display of the day.

Near the aircraft stood a mechanic in white overalls. He was looking neither at Grotte nor the ancient biplanes. His eyes constantly swept the area leading from the main buildings to a Royal Air Force VC10 which was obviously being held in readiness for some departing top brass.

As Gest pushed the wheel-chair up to the Cub, the mechanic nodded, "Take your time, gents," he said. "They haven't arrived yet."

"Get in, get started up and get clearance," Chiliman moved irritatedly in the wheelchair. "I want us out as quickly as possible. It's only a short hop over the frontier, but the quicker we do it the better."

"You had no trouble getting through, then?" queried the mechanic.

"I never have trouble getting through," Chiliman was lifting his bulk out of the wheel-chair, Gest going through the motions of helping him. "I haven't used the aircraft here for nearly six months, but they never forget me. The police are watching the commercial exits, now get moving."

"Ah," said the mechanic, "here they come, I think. Best be ready, Mr. Gest. I'll be back in a tick."

Plenty of police were ready to greet them inside the terminal building. Zizi held Boysie's hand tightly as the courtesies were exchanged, Edith looking sour in a pale blue lightweight suit.

There were posters everywhere advertising the air circus and Boysie perused one as Edith spoke with one of Couperose's men and an airport official. From the French he deciphered that the circus gave treats of great aeronautic nostalgia, including a dog fight with Baron von Himbeere and a demonstration with live ammunition fired into the water from a genuine relic RE 8.

"You ready, Oakes? They've sent a VC10." Edith all officious.

"Couldn't we hang about and see the air show?"

"You'll get all the air shows you want, lad. They're waiting to get us off so that they can begin the wretched air carnival. They work to a tight schedule here and apparently they've got a private light aircraft they have to get off as well."

Boysie shrugged and followed the others through the checkpoints, indulging in a couple of fantasies as they were saluted by French police officers.

As they emerged on the departure side of the terminal, Boysie's ears were filled with the roar of engines from the string and fabric aircraft lined up to the right, the three Nieuport 17s, the Fokker and the RE 8, all chugging and trembling away in discordant cacophony.

The VC10 stood lowering on the taxi track with its hatch open, the ramp out and a little WRAF stewardess waiting patiently.

"Come on, Oakes," snapped Edith, striding briskly towards the aircraft.

"We 'ad better go, Boyzee," Zizi tugged.

Boysie tore his eyes away and took two steps forward. Out of the corner of his eye he glimpsed a white figure coming round from behind the tail of the RE 8, the nearest aircraft. Something made him look back. The man was wearing overalls and when he saw Boysie had spotted him he raised an arm.

"Hey," Boysie muttered to Zizi, "Hey, it's Charlie Griffin."

"Sharlie," squeaked Zizi, and taking no notice of Edith they both turned towards their old murderous colleague.

"Where the bloody hell did you get to?" Boysie was only a few paces away from him now.

"Sorry, I haven't got time to explain now, Mr. Oakes. Really I'm sorry, but I have to take my work where I can find it and they do pay well. It's a pity really."

"What're you on about? ..." Boysie began.

"It's like a sort of parting shot, Mr. Oakes."

Then Boysie saw Griffin's gun hand come up. The sun, low across the Alps, glinted off the blue barrel of a wicked little automatic, and he could have sworn there were tears in Griffin's eyes.

Zizi screamed and there was a shout from Edith, now twenty yards away towards the RAF aircraft, the whole almost drowned by the backdrop of ancient engines.

XIX - AIR

A simple melody for voice or instrument (best played on a G String!)

Boysie braced himself to receive the bullet, but when the shot came it was from behind him and Griffin lurched to the left clutching his shoulder, the white overalls stained red.

Boysie glanced back to see William Edith struggling with a jammed Walther, the slide locked to the rear of the butt. Griffin had regained his balance, slewed around, sideways on. Boysie made a leap at him, low down in a rugger tackle which missed, leaving Boysie eating the tarmac while Griffin loped off behind the line of aircraft.

Pandemonium was breaking out from behind him, and as Boysie climbed to his feet, rubbing a knee, he saw Edith throwing his automatic pistol away in disgust. Against his better judgment, Boysie set off at a trot after Griffin, his mind churning and a gout of bitterness welling inside him, flowering into fury.

True he had used Griffin time and again, they had forged a relationship and that had been in his terrifying line of business. He should have known better than to trust the undertaker with his harmless little jokes and murderous intentions. Dogs and killers sometimes bite the hand that feeds them.

Griffin was well away, trotting in his loping lopsided stride towards the little Piper Cub which was already moving onto the taxi track. Boysie would never catch him on foot.

He stood there for a moment, helpless as Griffin swung himself up the wing and the Cub's engines rose to full power.

There was another face that Boysie recognised through the polished perspex hood: Caesar Chiliman glaring malevolently towards him.

Edith was beside him now. "Bloody thing jammed," Edith's voice rising to a falsetto. "Do something, Oakes. Don't just stand there. Do something and I'll get you off the hook. It's Chiliman and Gest as well."

For a frozen fragment of a second, Boysie held him full face, then he was moving, shouting back at Edith as he ran, the words bellowing from his throat in rage. "I told you to get your number dry, Edith. You need more experience, you need to get your nasty knees brown, more experience in the field. But I'll fix the sods for you, especially sodding Griffin. Sod them." He was dashing back along the rear of the parked air circus planes.

The pilot of the RE 8 was still in his cockpit, his observer standing by the aircraft, the engine idling, puffing exhaust from the twin pipes which ran at right angles from the fuselage carrying the fumes away over the upper wing.

Boysie clambered up the lower wing root, shouting in the pilot's ear, "Can you speak English?" Enunciating carefully and making each word count.

"My native tongue," the pilot shouted back. "I'm an Aussie, cobber."

Boysie pointed out through the whirling disc of the four-bladed propeller. "Can you catch that Cub?"

"Who wants to know?"

"I'm a British Intelligence officer," shouted Boysie, believing every word of it. "I've got to stop the bastards."

"Can but try, mate."

"Okay. Follow that Cub. The guns loaded?"

He looked back into the rear cockpit at the twin Lewis guns in their ring mounting, each with its drum magazine in place, the big circular sight rising between them.

"They're loaded okay, Blue, for the demo. Get in and I'll make this flying shithouse do things that'll turn Jonathan Livingston Seagull green with envy."

Boysie prised himself into the rear cockpit, unmercifully small and cramped. He felt he might also turn green, but not with envy. By this time, the Australian's observer was on the wing root and there was a lot of shouting going on, much swearing decorating the conversation. Then the observer threw a pair of goggles at Boysie, gave him the thumbs up sign and leaped down and under the aircraft.

He must have been pulling the chocks away, because, before Boysie could get the goggles over his head, the pilot had the throttle open and they were bumping and swaying forward. For a moment, Boysie remembered the fairground rides of his youth as the St. Giles' Fair made its round of the Berkshire towns.

The Cub was almost airborne, Boysie could see it starting to climb away from the main runway parallel with the sea. It was being pursued by a pair of police cars and a fire engine which were not likely to unstick and get into the air behind it.

The Australian did not seem to bother about minor details like runways, he just opened the engine and headed across the airfield, over the tarmac, apron, taxi track and earth, the old machine bouncing and juddering so that everything blurred and Boysie had the distinct impression that his joints would be telescoped one with another.

Then the propeller blades seemed to catch hold of the air as though they were boring through something solid, and they began to claw their way off, smoother now, though engulfed by noise and buffeted by the wind and slipstream howling around the open cockpit.

There was a whining in the wire stays between the wing struts and the ground fell away below them: with it went Boysie's stomach. From where he stood, in the tiny space set on top of the fuselage, he could see pieces of the fabric fluttering while the wings appeared to bend with the stress of air pressure. It was like riding a lawn mower high above the sea.

The Australian had unstuck her at a line which dissected the Cub's take-off path, cutting through at right angles. Now he was putting the aircraft into a tight turn, so that it tipped crazily as though they would be thrown down into the sea. It was at that moment Boysie realised that you normally carried parachutes in aeroplanes like this. He was without any visible means of support and did not relish the thought of what might happen if the pilot decided to try any advanced aerobatics. It was a long way down.

Boysie watched, trying not to look below him, as they grabbed at the air, throttle through the gate, urging upwards towards the Cub which had eased off on its climb, heading over the sea towards Italy.

The Cub, he presumed, had the edge on them as far as speed was concerned, but she also had a full load with Chiliman, Gest and the wounded Griffin up front, and her little 65hp engine would be flat out.

He was hypnotised, his eyes never leaving the Cub as it grew larger above their upper wing. At one point the Australian turned round, grinning, with his thumb stabbing upwards.

They appeared to inch up through the sky and it was almost with surprise that Boysie realised they were very close to the Piper Cub - so close that they were bucking and jigging in its slipstream.

The Australian turned again and pointed upwards making a movement with his hand which Boysie interpreted as a signal that they were going to climb above the other aircraft and come down level with them.

He nodded, turning his attention to the guns, aware for the first time that it was very cold and his hands, unprotected by gloves, were stiff and clumsy.

It was years since he had seen a Lewis gun, but the operation was relatively simple. He found the cocking handles on the right-hand sides of the guns, and the safety catches. Pushing between the weapons so that both butts rested easily into his shoulders, he grasped the grips and triggers.

The weapons swung in an easy arc on their ring mounting, the large circular metal sight with its crossed wires level with his eyes. Biggles and Ginger, he thought briefly, then the old RE 8 slewed to one side and the Piper Cub slid into vision. They were riding, lifting and falling like the ginny horses on a big roundabout, formatting with the little aircraft.

He could see clearly into the cabin. Griffin lying back, his face white and head lolling as though half conscious; Chiliman bulked beside him and the shape of Gest cramped at the controls, shooting nervous glances towards the RE 8.

Boysie's stomach lifted and dropped as the Australian waggled their wings ferociously, a hand out motioning downwards towards Chiliman. Boysie followed suit, panning the twin guns, traversing along the Cub's fuselage and then firmly moving them up and down.

He saw Chiliman's mouth open and close in a stream of abuse; a pudgy hand reaching out to slide back part of the canopy window; the hand coming up with a pistol. Then a whip and crack as a bullet ploughed into the fuselage between himself and the pilot.

The RE 8 dropped its nose violently and appeared to remain motionless, the Cub disappearing from view, lifting above them. An increasing whistling through the aircraft framework, then the roar of their motor and pressure, as though he was being forced back by an invisible hand. They were in a skidding turn to the right and then the left. Then a small, tight circle and the Cub was above and in front of them again.

When the Australian turned to look back at him this time he was not grinning, his finger crooked in a trigger-squeezing motion.

Boysie nodded. They climbed again, the Cub to their right. The pilot lifted a hand and slewed, yawing the aircraft, bringing the Cub's tail obliquely on to Boysie's cockpit.

He sighted quickly through the metal ring and pressed both of the triggers, but the tail was only there for a few seconds and the burst went wide.

The engine roared once more and they were again climbing over the Cub, losing a little distance. This time the Australian lined them up, above and to the left, throttle wide, before tipping the wings, flying tilted to one side.

Boysie had the rear of the Cub firmly in the sights now. He felt the Lewis guns come alive and pieces started flying from the Cub's fuselage just forward of the tail plane.

The Cub bucked, turned gently away, its belly exposed for a second, nose down, diving for the sea below. The Australian had their nose down, following, the wind banshee-howling and whipping in one long stream around them.

The Cub was performing a slow spiral, going down as though on an invisible and perfectly constructed set of rails. Twice she came through the gun sights and on both occasions Boysie managed a two-second burst. The second time more pieces fell away, then her nose settled down and the spiral stopped.

The RE 8 pulled up and they had a clear picture of the small aircraft as it hammered, gently it seemed, in a straight inevitable line towards the sea.

Far below, it hit with a flower of spray. Boysie distinctly saw the high wing break in two, one half go fluttering back to land skipping on the sea. Then they turned away and he could only see the mountains ahead, and below, along the coastline, the white sprawl of Nice and the rough dirty promontory that was the airport, the sea flecked with red from the sun setting gently behind the mountains.

XX - CODA

In musical analysis, a section of a movement considered to be added at the end as a rounding off rather than as a structural necessity

"No news of Griffin's body?"

William Edith shook his head.

It was six weeks and a lot of words later. They sat in the room which Boysie had once known well as the Chief's office, when he had worked for Special Security. The chair was now firmly occupied by William Edith, Number One of the Department of Tactical Security.

The various committees of investigation had done their work thoroughly enough, establishing that Griffin, along with a number of other well-known professional hired experts, had long been on Chiliman's list of operatives.

They also had irrefutable evidence that, on the night when Mostyn was killed in Paris, Griffin had walked calmly out of the hotel only seconds after the shooting had taken place. It was presumed that Lyric Lavenham had, of her own initiative, realised that this was the case. Griffin would have been forced, under these circumstances, to get rid of her. The details would never be available.

For Boysie the whole world had changed. Mostyn gone, Griffin revealed as a treacherous mercenary prepared to change sides for the highest bidder. He found that hard to accept, but it was fact and Griffin with whom he had worked for years, now lay at the bottom of the Mediterranean: they had recovered only Chiliman's body, bloated and thrown up on the coastline a week after the affair ended high over Nice. No trace of either Gest or Griffin.

Though second thoughts were inevitable, Zizi Portobello had taken Boysie at his word, and after so many years in happy and unrestrained bachelordom, the one-time Liquidator of Special Security was trapped, once and for all, at Marylebone Register Office one bright spring morning three weeks after the Piper Cub had sliced into the sea.

They had gone off, happy enough, for a couple of months' sun and sea in the comparative tranquillity of the Greek Islands, only to find Boysie summoned back to London after three weeks.

The cable had read: YOU ARE STILL A MEMBER OF THIS DEPARTMENT STOP URGENT YOU SHOULD REPORT HERE DAY AFTER TOMORROW STOP EDITH STOP

Boysie replied: CANNOT STOP STOP PHIZ OFF STOP STOP BOTHERING STOP OAKES STOP

Three hours later, two extremely large men arrived at their secluded hotel and suggested that unpleasant things might happen if Boysie did not return to London.

By the time they got back to Heathrow, Zizi had mollified her husband, and Boysie, true to form, arrived at Edith's office with his resignation neatly typed in his breast pocket.

"How is the fair Mrs. Oakes?" asked Edith, strangely pleasant.

"She'll be okay once we can get back to the honeymoon," Boysie grinned placidly.

"The honeymoon is over," Edith showed his fangs. Boysie shook his head. "Wrong. My resignation." The paper fluttered onto the desk where Edith let it lie for a moment before picking it up gently and tearing it into pieces.

"There is no way," he smiled. "Once in you cannot get out, and you know it, Oakes. Besides I have your new appointment here."

Boysie picked it up with diffidence. His name was at the top of the list:

Brian Ian Oakes appointed deputy to William Frederick Frances St. John Edith, MBE. Special Duties.

His jaw dropped, "What the hell ...?"

"It means you're my Number Two. Mrs. Oakes should be pleased you're in work. Second-in-Command of Tactical Security is ample reward for the service you have done. It's also a demanding job. After all you have the experience. Congratulations."

"But I ... But I ... But I ..."

"You know where your office is. Downstairs. The one Mostyn used to use in the old days. I believe you have some interviewing to do. There are a couple of applicants for the training course."

Half an hour later, having haltingly called Zizi, Boysie sat behind the desk which had for so long been used in the old days by Colonel James

George Mostyn. The longer he sat there the more he tasted the power that was now his. It was not an unpleasant sensation.

A tap on the door called forth a dazed "Come in," and a tall willowy blonde with magnificent contours entered clutching a shorthand pad. She had eyes which beckoned Boysie to darkened rooms and soft silk sheets.

"The applicants are here, sir," she said.

Boysie knew instinctively that she was really telling him that she would be free after hours for whatever he had in mind. The thought of Zizi, alone in the Ken High Street flat, dragged him back to reality.

"Wheel the first one in then, love, and, oh, what did you say your name was?"

"I didn't, sir, but it's Iris."

He felt a flicker low down in his loins.

"My private number is in the file, sir," she vamped.

"Wheel the first one in," Boysie picked up the dossier which lay in front of him.

The first one was a tall man, bronzed, obviously fit and muscular. He had light blue eyes and the left side of his mouth had a tendency to twitch upwards.

"Come in, laddie," said Boysie. "Come in and sit down." His voice sounded almost smarmy.

Acknowledgments

I am often accused, quite unjustifiably, of not giving credit where credit is due. In order to avoid the wrath of those concerned, I now list the following acknowledgments for this, the eighth, Boysie Oakes Entertainment:

Patience by Hodder & Stoughton

Odd Quips by Alexis and Simon Gardner

Typing by Margaret Gardner

Flight Information by Capt. E. Mercer, D.F.C.

Enthusiasm by Simon Wood

Constant Harassment by Alexis and Simon Gardner and their friends, also recordings of numerous pop groups

Mr. Oakes' Dreams at Chalon-sur-Saône by Ann Evans

Typewriters by Adler and Olympia

Miss Lavenham and Mlle. Portobello's Wardrobes by Mr. Gardner's roving eye

Chapter Headings mainly by courtesy of *A New Dictionary of Music*

Wigs by Christopher Worner

Cigarettes by John Player

Nerve by John Gardner

16357142R00093

Printed in Great Britain
by Amazon